Love
at the
Salted Caramel
Cafe

Angie Ellington

Angie Ellington

ISBN:9781719976725

Cover Art © canva.com & istock
with purchased digital use rights

Acknowledgments
Thank you for your support. Dedicated to my family and friends.

Work of Fiction
This book is a work of fiction. The names, characters, places, and incidents are products of the writer's imagination or have been used fictitiously and are not to be construed as real. Any resemblance to persons, living or dead, actual events, locales, or organizations is entirely coincidental.

TABLE OF CONTENTS

Chapter 1
Chapter 2
Chapter 3
Chapter 4
Chapter 5
Chapter 6
Chapter 7
Chapter 8
Chapter 9
Chapter 10
Chapter 11
Chapter 12
Chapter 13
Chapter 14
Chapter 15
Chapter 16
Chapter 17
Chapter 18
Chapter 19
Chapter 20
Chapter 21
Chapter 22
Epilogue
More from the Author
Sample of Christmas in Frost Bend

CHAPTER ONE

Sierra Blake pulled into the small graveled parking lot outside of The Salted Caramel Cafe. A quaint establishment renamed after winning multiple regional and state awards for caramel concoctions. She watched an elderly couple making their way up the side entrance a few feet in front of her, as the man held his wife steady. She was using the wooden ramp's rail for additional support, donning a small burgundy hat with a yellow bird attached to the side. A long black dress swayed along her weathered ankles brushing over black orthopedic sneakers. She had a yellow shawl that matched the bird on the hat draped over her shoulders in perfect symmetry on either shoulder.

As they reached the door, a handsome young man in his twenties held the door open and assisted them inside. The older gentleman removed his Fedora hat that completed his suit of full light gray, and as he turned to the side upon entering, Sierra spotted a small yellow handkerchief tucked neatly in his shirt pocket. No tie, but he still found a way to match his wife's attire, or possibly she had insisted upon the match.

Sierra wondered if they had been to a wedding, a church function, or possibly a funeral. It was the start of a Saturday afternoon in Mill Hollows, so any of those were possible. She knew much of the small town she had grown up in hadn't and wouldn't change. It was a predictable weekend of calendar events, she was sure. She had noticed the fruit stand had the usual gathering next to it as she turned onto the street behind the cafe.

She had heard roars from the men watching a football game playing at Frankie's Brewhaus a little further down as she came to a halt at the stoplight. It was certainly Virginia Tech against a popular rival team, as college football in a town located within a half hour of the popular university created a reason for gathering together, consuming beer, and trading criticisms about the other teams. It was their version of a book club.

Sierra shut off the engine of her silver Audi SUV, inhaling a full breath as she looked in the rearview mirror. She brushed her hair back out of her face. She had been driving for five hours after an overnight stay at a friend's house from college and had let her window down when she came into Mill Hollows to feel the breeze upon her face in the 25-speed zone, soaking in the early Autumn combination of warm and cool air as they collided for domination.

Sierra glanced over to the sports bar that was now in view as she exited her vehicle. She saw a small crowd standing in the doorway. A burly man in a full beard confirmed her assumption that it was a college football game causing the boisterous voices, as he leaned forward, tucked his elbows inward, and began some type of odd chicken dance in his Virginia Tech sweatshirt. Sierra assumed Tech must have won the game or at least have scored a touchdown and were making a comeback. She shook her head and began to snicker as she casually waved toward the heavily bearded chicken-dancing man. The happy, and possibly slightly intoxicated football fan, stopped his dance long enough to wave and yell "Ho---kieeesss" as Sierra gave two thumbs up and widened her mouth in a large smile.

Growing up in a home of Hokies fans and having her younger brother play football there in college, she still enjoyed seeing the revelry and joy it seemed to bring out in the community. Although Sierra never got into football on a live-eat-breathe level, she had been a cheerleader for her high school football team and was the daughter of the coach. High school football games on Friday nights. College football on Saturdays, either at home or in the stands of the Hokies stadium. Sundays? Well, Sundays were for church and family lunches.

The argument that football was only seasonal didn't hold water as Sierra recalled her mother saying, against family Sundays of church services, big meals, and evenings with one set or the other of grandparents.

This was a typical Saturday in October for the town that could easily be the subject of a Norman Rockwell painting to a tourist passing through. Well, maybe not quite that lovely, but Mill Hollows was pretty close to the best place to call home as anywhere else Sierra could compare it to. She had missed this place. These people.

She walked up to the cafe door, raising her sunglasses on her head above her loosely twisted dark blonde hair that she had brushed free from a top knot that had fallen almost free from the drive through town.

The handsome younger man opened the door for another older couple who were on their way out when he caught Sierra's half-uncertain, half-giddy, start of a smile as she approached the sign to the cafe and the sidewalk.

"Sierra?! Are you really here?" The dark-haired man now beamed with delight as they embraced.

"Yes, baby brother. I'm really here. I've missed you so much, Tom-Tom." They both laughed.

"Only you would still call your twenty-four-year-old brother, Tom-Tom," he said slightly blushing with embarrassment. "Come on to the back. Roxie is working the afternoon shift today."

Sierra pulled back from her brother. "I don't want to bother her while she's working. I know how busy the cafe gets on Saturdays. Mom keeps me informed. She says Roxie is doing well managing the place. I'm glad."

They exchanged awkward glances toward the kitchen.

"I just wanted to stop by and see the place for a minute on my way to the house. I don't think I'm ready to see Roxie just yet; nor do I think she will be as pleased to see me as you are. Thank you, little brother, for....well, just being the sweetheart you've always been. I love you kiddo!" Sierra gave Tom a little punch on the shoulder.

"I love you, too. I wish you and Roxie would mend whatever fence has been broken between you two. Neither of you will talk about whatever happened with me and Mom feels caught in the middle. Dad, of course, just doesn't talk about anything unless he has to, but I'm sure he would have quite a bit to say to both of you if you probed him for advice," Tom added policing for information from his oldest sibling.

"Look at you becoming so wise. You must have learned *something* at Virginia Tech. Lord knows you didn't spend much time attending classes from what you would tell me in the rare texts I would receive mid-afternoon when you had just rolled out of bed. We'll catch up tonight. I'll see you at the house."

Sierra grabbed a chocolate brownie from the sample table. "Yum. Carlotta made these, didn't she?" Sierra quickly wiped her lip with a napkin as Tom grinned at the chocolate and pointed to the corner of Sierra's mouth.

"Yep, you know Roxie doesn't do the baking. You're the one who inherited the baking gene for sure. I'm learning how to smoke meats and a few other things, but the desserts mom could make a cookbook out of definitely aren't going to be prepared by Roxie. She's very good at *being in charge*, though," Tom replied with a snide grin.

"Oh yes, I'm certain she has no trouble keeping everyone in line, if she doesn't cause them to quit first. Amazingly, she hasn't lost Carlotta yet. I guess mom has given her the warning of where the line is drawn," Sierra added.

"Yeah, well, she's had seven or eight employees walk off the job since she took over running the cafe, but I guess in two years, that isn't that bad of a ratio for turnover."

They both snickered.

"I'll see you tonight. Sneak me a full-sized brownie if there are any left, will ya?" Sierra touched Tom's shoulder and patted him.

"Bye, sis. Anything for you after all the bowls and spoons you let me sample when

Mom and Dad said no sugar near dinner."
They hugged again as Sierra grabbed another
brownie sample. Tom cocked his head and
raised his brow as his sibling covered the
brownie bite with a napkin.

"What?" Sierra asked, bobbing her
shoulder with a curled lip and a wink.

"This bite is for Mom." Sierra waved as
she scurried past the window outside and
popped the brownie in her mouth. She tried
not to laugh with a filled cheek as Tom tapped
on the window from inside the cafe and threw
his hand up.

CHAPTER TWO

The sun was shining brightly above the trees bursting through with light beams illuminating the rich leaves. At sunset, the light blue sky would be ablaze as it merged with the firestorm of rich colors surrounding the Blake's property in the heart of Mill Hollows. Sierra sat in her SUV in awe of the changing leaves and breezes blowing them around in a dance; a sight she hadn't seen in some time.

Since moving to Tampa, she had longed for changing seasons that she had taken for granted. The summer temps and humidity that rarely took a break were beginning to bore her, although before moving to Florida a few years earlier, she would never have imagined she'd tire of wearing shorts and flip-flops year-round.

She closed her eyes and felt her fallen hair softly blow across her cheek, as the breeze tickled her eyelashes.

Must I get out or could I possibly sit here

for hours and avoid all thoughts other than those brought on by the sound of leaves rustling and descending gently upon my car?

She was tired from the drive, but the comfort of sitting in silence was about so much more than sleep deprivation. She felt at peace in Mill Hollows. A peace that she knew would be fleeting in only a matter of time.

Leaving home and choosing to pursue a career of her own after her mother became ill was not a well-received decision by everyone in the Blake family. Sierra had come home as often as possible during her mother's treatments and recovery periods; whenever she was permitted time off, but she wasn't able to be there for some of the most difficult days. That had hurt Sierra so deeply that after her mother's recovery, she didn't visit as often as she could have. There was such guilt in her heart, and she knew her mother wasn't the only one she felt guilty towards.

Time had healed some of the tension and resentment, but the distance had kept confrontation at bay. The few days she had returned for holidays and special occasions had allowed for temporary pleasantries and hollowed smiles. Although Miranda Blake had always supported and encouraged her children to make their own way in life, not all of her children felt they were treated equally.

Sierra's younger brother, Tom, was the baby of the family, and the athlete. He was much too busy and unfamiliar with the chaos and frustrations that arose during his mother's battle with breast cancer. He was in his sophomore year of college when she began her treatments. Miranda Blake had insisted that her son remain in school and the family agreed to keep him in the dark during the worst of days. Miranda did her best to fight through the pain and lethargy during his time at home and sheltered him as much as possible.

He was a good kid. Star running-back of his high school football team and a top player at Virginia Tech. Richard Blake had dreams for his only son to become a football coach, and follow in his footsteps. He knew Tom wasn't quite strong enough of a college player to pursue a career in the NFL, even if they did their best to make him feel like a star. Staying grounded was also a must in the Blake household. Richard never missed a game; even when Miranda was having a difficult weekend, as she insisted one of them be there to support their youngest child.

Oftentimes, Sierra's younger sister, Roxie, was left to care for her mother, handle family affairs, and run the cafe that her mother owned. It had been Miranda's wish since she was a teenager to one day own a cafe and had become not only her pride and joy, outside of her family but an outlet for creativity that gave her a sense of pride and accomplishment.

She prided herself in her role as a mother

and wife, but she relished in pleasing locals and travelers who would stop in for a meal and rave about the latest dishes and baked goods.

When she became ill, she was devastated at the thought of letting the cafe go, as it kept her motivated during her lowest points of depression. She would work when she could, as often as her body would allow, and when she couldn't, her middle child, Roxie, and Carlotta, her right-hand cafe employee, and friend, would pitch in and do the best they could to keep customers happy, and Miranda comforted.

The family was very fortunate that Miranda had recovered and won her battle against cancer. She had gone through a double mastectomy, chemotherapy, and reconstruction. No signs of cancer had appeared in the past two years, after a year and a half battle, that they all knew she was lucky to have defeated. They prayed it wouldn't return and were thankful she was gradually regaining her joy in new ways outside of the cafe. Joining a gym and volunteering at the town's makeshift museum had become more fun than the cafe and she was happy to step back...a little.

Still, the depressive state the disease had left her in lingered from time to time. Beating cancer wasn't the only battle that came from having it. She had returned to work at the cafe, but some days; some weeks even, she would continue to struggle to find her energy and positive spirit that went into making the Salted Caramel Cafe the popular dining spot that it was.

Sierra knew she should have offered to come home and run the cafe, but Roxie was there. Although Sierra had been a natural in the kitchen with her mother, it made sense for Roxie to take over temporarily. It was supposed to be only temporary. Miranda wouldn't hear of it, as Sierra was working as a hotel manager in Tampa, and was only at the beginning of a successful future there. It would be a career pitfall too early on, according to Miranda. Sierra had only been in Florida for a year when her mother was diagnosed for the first time. By the second round, she had been offered a management position with a well-known resort.

She had studied business with a concentration in hospitality management in college at Radford, had spent years in dead-end jobs in neighboring cities in low-end hotels, and restaurants, and had worked two jobs most of the time to make ends meet. It was the perfect job for Sierra in her field if she wanted to relocate, and her mother recalled how elated Sierra was at the opportunity. She had been blissfully happy in Tampa. There was no way Miranda Blake would allow her daughter to give that up.

***

Sierra awoke to a tap on her shoulder. Her father had walked up from the shed behind her. He had been reorganizing tools and cleaning up the storage room. Something he did once a year on a cool fall day.

"Well, are ya going to sit there and nap all afternoon or get out and give your ol' dad a hug?" Richard asked as he opened the door to the Audi and took a step back for Sierra to get out. They shared a lengthy hug in silence while the breeze blew Sierra's hair around her dad's face.

"I've missed ya, Dad," Sierra said almost in a whisper. She knew her father had wanted her to move back during her mother's illness, but had respected Miranda's wishes and not pressed her to do so. Sierra felt a tear roll down her cheek, as every time she came home for a visit, she felt regret, despite her many offers to move home in the past. This time, the sadness was part of something more.

Her parents knew she was coming home, but no one else did. She hadn't said why; just that she needed a break and some time at home. She knew not everyone would be happy to see her, but the time had come to say things that needed to be said and mend fences or possibly tear them down permanently. Which scenario would win out was anyone's guess.

CHAPTER THREE

"Randa. Randaaa!" Richard called out in search of his wife. "That dang woman can disappear faster than the last ham biscuit at breakfast. I swear she was laying on the couch with Poppy watching one of those Lifetime movies where some woman's twin was pretending to be her and fooling the husband into thinking she was his wife or something crazy like that. It makes a man nervous to see his wife watching too many movies about cheating and stalkers and such. If she's not watching that channel, it's those mystery series movies....oh, what's her favorite? Oh, darn. Wait a second. It's on the tip of my tongue. Shoot. Anyway, they've got desserts in the title." Richard trailed off as he walked toward the back of the house. "Randa, you back here?"

Sierra chuckled as her dad rounded the kitchen towards the office room. He always teased them about watching *silly* movies, but he knew enough about them to tell people the gist of the plot and some of the character details, so he gave it away that he secretly liked to watch them without appearing as though he did. He would work on a crossword puzzle in the recliner that he would only manage to partially complete in two hours when he could complete crosswords faster than most if he were paying attention.

Miranda rather enjoyed it. She didn't mind his grumpy complaining about her movies, because she would do the same when his westerns and old action movies were on. She secretly liked to keep up with a little of what was going on with those movies and shows, as well but would knit on the couch while he watched. Sierra was glad to see that her dad was still the same in that respect. It made it feel like a little less time had passed.

Miranda came into the living room, giddy and almost jumping as she scooted quickly across the kitchen, almost sliding into the living room on the hardwood floors.

"Sierra, I'm so happy you're home, honey!" Miranda pulled her daughter into a tight and warm embrace, pulling back to give a kiss on the cheek and returning to the full hug position.

"I'm happy to be home, mom. I've missed you." Miranda spun around and pointed to Richard.

"Turn the oven off, Richard. Those peanut butter cookies you wanted are going to burn otherwise." Richard did as he was instructed.

The cookies wouldn't have burned. No

matter what multitasking activities Miranda Blake had going on, she would never forget to turn off the oven for something she was cooking or baking up. When she was unable to work at the cafe, in some ways that was harder than battling the cancer because being a chef and baker was what kept her sane, as she would often say. Even during her hardest days, she wanted to hear about the cafe and Roxie would oblige. If the cafe was having any trouble that day, she would try her best to sugarcoat it and only tell positive details, but Miranda had a sixth sense about the cafe and the ability to always know when one of her children was lying. Each person had a *tell* and Roxie's *tell* was to fidget with her ring. She inherited their grandmother's ring when she was twelve and if she was ever trying to spin a story, so to speak, she would fumble around with the ring on her finger.

"So, we're glad you're home, of course, but you sounded a bit distressed on the phone. Is everything alright, dear?" Miranda wasted no time getting to the point of things. Sierra knew that she would probe her for information upon her arrival, so she was prepared with a starter story.

"I just miss my family. I've had a hectic few months at the hotel. Changes in principal management and some employee turnover that's been a bit of an adjustment. It's all par for the course in this industry, but lately, it's just more frustrating for me to deal with the added stress than it used to be. I just needed a little break. No big deal. I have some vacation time from last year that was left over, so I decided to take a two-week leave."

This was mostly true. She did technically get a severance package, which included two weeks of remaining vacation leave. However, Sierra had a *tell*, as well. She would take her hair down and swirl it back up into a clip or ponytail during her conversation when something wasn't quite fully true or when she was uncomfortable with dealing with emotional topics. Sierra had always been more reserved with her emotions. Toying with her hair had become synonymous with nervous energy or awkward conversations. Anything that made her heart rate palpitate at the speed of a football player going for a touchdown. Though emotional detachment had served her well in management, it had caused more than her share of heartache in her personal life.

How do I even begin to explain that I turned down a proposal from Miles? I've made him sound as perfect as if I'd had him custom-made in a factory of custom Ken dolls. I wanted him to be perfect. I needed him to be. In many ways, he was as I described to my family. Looks that rivaled a younger John Stamos. That was how I described him to my mother, at least so she would have someone of her celebrity dreams to compare him to. A lucrative career ahead.

Polite and courteous...well, usually. Oh, how I wanted him to be the man of my dreams. And I truly thought he was going to be.

"We were hoping you'd bring Miles with you to visit. You've been dating him for over a year now. When do we get to meet him? The wedding? You know we're not one of those hipster families who are comfortable with you marrying someone we've never met," Miranda affirmed with a raise of her brow. Sierra feigned a smile.

"Now, Randa. She's been here for all of five minutes and you're corralling her like a herd of cattle into the barn," Richard said, folding his arms over his pot belly and leaning back into his chair.

"Oh, hush up. I'm just curious about our oldest daughter's life along the warm and sunny beaches of Florida. I'm living vicariously a bit through her," Miranda retorted and brushed her hand toward Richard's direction.

Sierra swayed her eyes between them. This banter was nothing new. She had expected this precise conversation to ensue upon her arrival.

"I stopped by the cafe on my way in," Sierra said to divert the topic she was not ready to discuss. Her return-to-single status would come up again soon enough and she wanted to delay it as long as possible. "I saw Tommy."

"Was there a good crowd? How was the

bakery display window? Were there enough caramel scones and pumpkin cookies?" Miranda asked, as she leaned forward on the couch and touched Sierra's knee.

"Mom, calm down. Everything was fine, I'm sure. I didn't take inventory in the couple of minutes I was there, but yes, there were a few people and things appeared to be running smoothly, I guess," Sierra replied with a return touch over her mother's hand.

"You've got to let Roxie handle it if she's managing now, Mom."

Miranda blew out a heavy breath. "I know. I am giving her a try, but it's hard to let her have full control. It wasn't her choice or mine. You know it was only supposed to be for a while until we found out if I would..well, be able to return. Even though I beat the cancer, my energy just isn't what it once was. I still go to the cafe a few times per week for a few hours, but I'm not sure if Roxie is up for the task of running it full-time. Tom helps out occasionally on weekends, but he's so busy with coaching football and then basketball for the high school that it must be more of a burden on him than he admits."

Richard pulled the handle and opened the recliner to a comfortable position.

"Now, we've talked about this with both of them. Tommy wants to help out. Besides, he knows his older sister needs guidance, and a spy who'll run back and report any mischief to you keeps Roxanne on her toes. It's not a burden. It's family. It's what we do for family. I help out. Sierra worked there, too. Heck. Sierra was ready to run the cafe when she was around twelve, weren't ya darlin'?" Richard let out a raspy cackle and a warm smile covered all of their faces.

"I loved the cafe. It was my escape from the awkwardness that was my life back then. Having braces for what felt like a decade, being in the band playing the flute, and preferring to spend Saturday nights baking with mom rather than hanging out at the old mill with most everyone else from high school," Sierra said and shrugged. "Those memories are so special to me. You know if I were here, I'd have taken over the cafe for you, but I'm sure Roxie is doing well in the role. Right?"

Sierra made a sour face as she exchanged similar glances with her parents. "I mean, Roxie didn't love the cafe as I did, but she loves you, Mom. She'd do anything for you. So, I'm sure she's doing her best." She swallowed hard, hoping she sounded convincing and knowing it wasn't likely.

"Roxie does her best. You're right. I'm not saying she doesn't put the effort in, but your sister has so much on her plate in her personal life. Some days are harder than others. Her heart has never been in the kitchen or in running a business. You were always more interested in both." Miranda lowered her chin and took a sip from a glass of water that had been sitting on the coffee table.

"I only want my kids to be happy. All of you. I'm so glad you're here for a visit, honey."

Sierra's mouth curved upward and she nodded. "Me too." After a few minutes of watching football on the television and watching her dad call out the referees twice, Sierra rose from the couch, tugging her low-hung jeans up around her hips. "I'm going to go unpack and take a shower. It's been a long drive," she said.

"Sure, dear. I'm certain Poppy is already laying across the bed on your suitcase waiting for you," Miranda replied with a chuckle.

"I was wondering why she hadn't been in here to see me yet. That cat loves a suitcase more than a human, though. If it were open, she'd be tucked in a ball inside of it shedding yellow fur on my clothes," Sierra added with a giggle.

She entered the bedroom that she once shared with her younger sister. There was now a single full-sized bed inside for her visits home or when Roxie had needed refuge for a few days or weeks during one of her break-ups with Toby. Sierra could still picture the two twins she had shared with her sister, who were often pushed together when Roxie was little and afraid of any noise coming from the hallway.

A stout Garfield clone of a feline with an attitude to match stretched her claws out over Sierra's navy and orange travel bag.

"Poppy!" Sierra scolded. "Get your claws out of my bag. It's not your scratching post, chunky monkey." She sat on the lavender and gray comforter as her furry sibling rolled over and yawned. Sierra's lips curved upward and she sighed with a chuckle. "Oh, Poppy," she said as she began rubbing the cat's ears and chin. "You are still the queen of the castle." Poppy burrowed against Sierra's hand.

CHAPTER FOUR

Sierra returned from showering to find Poppy had migrated over and curled up snugly across her sweatshirt. It warmed her heart to see the cat's paw curled over the sleeve. She wished she had time for a pet. With her schedule, she didn't spend much time in her swanky eighth-floor apartment overlooking Old Tampa Bay.

Between traveling for hotel conventions and management training, and of course long days and nights at the resort she worked for, there wasn't much time for herself. She rarely had spent much time with Miles during their relationship. All the more reason to convince herself that he was the perfect boyfriend. His adversity to cats as shedders who only want attention and do not return it had not sat well with her, but as she didn't have a pet, she had allowed that as a flaw she'd disregard.

As she rubbed Poppy, she thought about that comment and other similar negative remarks about pets Miles had made early in their relationship.

I should've known then. A man who doesn't appreciate cats, and isn't even an enthusiast of dogs, needs a higher ranking on my pro/con list as a deal-breaking con.

Sierra perused pictures hanging on the walls as her toffee brown eyes began to moisten. She moved closer to a 5x7 framed image on the top of a hope chest and lifted it into her hand. It was a faded image of her and Roxie sitting on their father's knee one year when he had volunteered to serve as Santa Claus for a church fundraiser for underprivileged youth in Mill Hollows. Something he did for a few years when they were little. Sierra's cheeks tightened and a salty taste filled her mouth. She was inseparable from her younger sibling of three years back then.

Miranda entered the doorway and leaned against it quietly; watching her oldest child with adoration. Sierra had become a successful woman. She had made her mother so proud. Her wish was that she was closer to home, but she knew Mill Hollows didn't offer much in the way of careers worthy of Sierra's academic achievements. Although Miranda had secretly hoped Sierra would take over the cafe someday, she had never discouraged her from pursuing her career goals.

"That's one of my favorite photos of the three of you," Miranda spoke softly. Sierra flinched with surprise and turned to face her mother. She forced a softer smile across her face. "Roxanne was never far from your side back then," Miranda continued. "I was pregnant with Tommy, and I remember the two of you in pigtails kissing my belly every night when I tucked you in your beds." She placed her hands over her heart and a joyful chuckle opened her lips into a widened smile.

"I know, Mom. You've told us that story many times. I don't know how you and Dad raised three kids. I can't imagine getting one to turn out Okay. We certainly didn't look like this perfect photo by the time we were teenagers. I'm sorry for driving you nuts. I know playing referee between two hormonal teenage girls who couldn't even agree on which end of the couch to sit on was no picnic. I can still hear Dad bellowing out to us to sit on the floor one night because we were complaining over who had the better view of the TV from the couch," Sierra said with a roll of her eyes.

She walked over and hugged her mother, tightly, then eased the hold against her mother's thinner frame than she once had. Although Miranda Blake had beaten the war against breast cancer, she had her share of battle scars from the fight. Some had healed, such as hair loss and sickness from the chemo. Yet, her body was still rather frail and her amber-brown eyes didn't catch the light with the same sparkle they once had.

"Whoa!" Miranda said with a chortle. She

tapped her oldest around the center of her back. "I love you, darlin'. She rubbed Sierra's long golden blonde hair. "My beautiful eldest with hair as lovely as a caramel latte."

As they released their arms from each other, Miranda put her hand underneath Sierra's chin; angling it upward. "Is everything alright, sugar?"

Sierra breathed in deeply. "It's fine, mom. I wanted to hug my mommy. Sometimes, you just need to do that. Doesn't matter how old you get. I love that you still tell us our hair looks like coffee and dessert blends. Unless Roxie has changed hers again, she's still a buttercream muffin."

Miranda nodded. "Yes. She's still light blonde. For now." She tilted her head slightly and peered into her daughter's saddened eyes. "When you're ready to tell me what's going on and not dodge the subject, let me know." She tapped her finger on Sierra's nose. "I know my children and a mother knows when something is wrong."

Sierra nodded and followed her mother down the hall and into the kitchen.

"Tom called me on my cell. He's coming over to help me get Roxie's stuff out. Deputy Wilkes is coming with him in case there's any trouble. I told him if that lowlife S-O-B sets foot on my property, there's definitely gonna be some trouble. I'm the property owner and he'd be trespassin'. If he makes a move to lay a hand on my daughter, they can come to take him away in a body bag," Richard lamented as he poured iced tea into a glass.

"Now, Richard, don't you go over there half-cocked and do anything stupid. We don't need you getting locked up. Let the Sheriff's deputies handle Toby. That's why Deputy Wilkes is coming. He's on duty, right?" Miranda probed.

"Yeah, he's on duty. Randa, what do you think I did? Hire him as a hitman?"

"I told Roxie you were picking up Eden from the birthday party at the skating rink down in Wayside Village. Take her to the cafe for a cookie or something," Richard added.

"Sierra, you wanna come with us? We could use an extra set of hands in getting his junk out. We're sending it with Jake to the jail. He can pick it up there. He ain't got much, but we don't want him to have a reason to come back here this time."

Sierra's face formed a mouth-opening, furrowed brow expression of confusion.

"What...is...happening? I thought Roxie broke up with Toby and he had moved into a camper on his uncle's farm or something. She took him back, again? This makes what...the fifth or sixth time she's kicked him out since Eden was born? I can't keep track. She'll just take him back again. She always does." Sierra folded her arms and hardened her expression. "I'm not getting involved, Dad. Sorry. Roxie and I...well, you know she doesn't want me involved in her life in any way that doesn't concern you two or Tom. It may be worse if I'm there. I'll go with Mom to get Eden. I'm not ready to see Roxie today."

"Well, honey. I suggest you both *get* ready. She's living here now. She and Eden are staying in Tommy's room. She knows you're coming. I had her move some things so the two of you can stay holed up in your rooms and avoid each other as much as you wish," Richard asserted.

"If Toby's out of the cabin, why aren't they staying there like they usually do?" Sierra questioned as she moved into the kitchen and poured a glass of water from the sink over ice.

"If she's here, perhaps he won't be able to convince her he's changed and show up at the cabin begging her to take him back like he's done every other time. She's ready to be done with him, Sierra. I know she's taken him back many times, but this time I think she wants it to stick. He went too far," Miranda added as she exchanged looks of concern with Richard.

"Now, Randa. That's not our story to tell when our girls need to work out some things," Richard said sternly.

Miranda waved her hands and teetered her head around.

Great. I can't escape the Hee-Haw show that is my life. Less than four hours in Mill Hollows and there's already a deputy assisting our family in keeping the peace and two grown women in their late twenties are going to be living with their parents again. I can hardly wait to drop the bomb that I lost my job when I turned down a proposal from Mr. Perfect. Mr. Perfect, who wanted to turn me into a baby factory and quit my job to, as he worded it, put my awesome baking skills to good use because of the free time I'd have. I'm no expert, but I don't know many moms of three or four kids who have time to bake cupcakes all day. Then, there's the timing of his proposal. In front of the entire board of the resort chain; including his parents!

CHAPTER FIVE

Leaves floated into a tango with the breeze along the winding road as Sierra and Miranda drove into Mill Hollows. The Blake's property was located a short distance outside of town on a hillside with the mountains of southern Virginia canvassing their backyard's skyline. Sierra stared out of the passenger window at the rustle of leaves and swaying song of the tree branches admiring the beauty of her hometown's countryside. She had missed the changing of seasons most of all while living in Florida.

Palm trees and temps in the eighties lasted most of the year in Tampa. The navy knitted sweater coat and leather boots over faded skinny jeans, layered over the buttercream tank she had comfortably slid into wasn't a look she would be wearing in Tampa on a typical afternoon any time of year. Long tanks and Capri leggings would be her casual choice even in December.

As they pulled into the graveled lot of the cafe, Sierra tucked her hands into the pockets of her sweater. The cool breeze fluttered through her long hair like butterflies in spring landing along the flowers. She breathed in the freshness of the valley air as she opened the back door and assisted Eden in getting out of her booster seat.

Eden wrapped her arms around Sierra's leg and held on tightly. Sierra felt her heart warm with glee.

"Okay. I can't move, Eden. You're too big to carry now," Sierra teased.

"You stay Aunt Rie. You stay wif me!" Eden bellowed out with demanding sweetness. She eased her grip and took Sierra's hand instead. The love of a little girl who thought she was the greatest aunt in the world gave her a pang of regret over not being closer to watch her niece as she grew.

"I wish I could stay with you all the time, Eden," Sierra said gently. "I'm here now and we're going to have some fun. I'm going to be here for a while."

"Goodie. We play wif my barbies?" Eden's face lit up with joy.

"Yes. We will certainly play with your Barbies, sweet girl."

They followed Miranda inside the cafe and toward the back to find Tom and Carlotta cleaning up the workstations and preparing for closing. A young teenager was serving a few last-minute customers having coffee and chicken salad sandwiches with pumpkin mashed potatoes. A specialty for the fall at the cafe.

"Hey, mom. Sis. Come here, Eden. Uncle T's got something I saved for you in this box," Tom said with an energetic bounce toward his niece.

"I believe *I* saved the something you're referring to for her," Carlotta corrected with a throated cough and a scowl that quickly switched into a jovial eye wink.

Eden bounced up and down in her tiny brown suede Ugg boots. A gift from Sierra the Christmas before. Her curly pigtails of platinum blonde bobbed along with her feet as she beamed.

"What is it Uncle T? Bwownie?" she asked in her high-pitched voice with the sweetness of child wonderment that would make the hardest of hearts soften like butter.

They all smiled and watched as Tom removed an orange cake pop with a vanilla cake filling from a container.

"Spwinkles!" Eden bellowed out with glee.

"Yes, honey. It has sprinkles on it. Your favorite," Miranda said.

Eden hugged Tom and then snuggled up around Carlotta's thickened hips as she rose from a chair and squeezed.

"Oh, Okay, Princess. You go enjoy your treat," Carlotta said almost breathlessly from the grip Eden still had around her thigh as she slid down her leg.

Tom led Eden to a small table in the corner of the baking room and headed out the back to join Richard and Roxie at the cabin. Miranda and Carlotta discussed the usual rundown of questions Miranda had when she came into the cafe. Discussions of the weekly specials, desserts, and how busy it had been that day. She would save a review of the expenses and receipts from the last week for Roxie.

Carlotta joined the waitress up front in preparing for closure as the couple that had been dining paid their bill. Sierra watched with attentive focus at everything surrounding her in the cafe. Marketing ideas swirled through her mind. She couldn't help it. Marketing was her forte' and she was good at it. It didn't fulfill her the way it did when she first started out working in hospitality marketing after graduation. Perhaps looking for a new position wasn't going to be such a bad thing after all. She hated being unemployed, but she hadn't been given much of a choice.

How does one continue working for a resort after turning down a wedding proposal from the manager and future owner of the hotel?

She could've accepted a transfer, but she didn't feel as though she deserved to be shipped off to the Gulf Coast to a smaller resort and lower stature in management. Besides, Miles had wanted her out. She had embarrassed him and embarrassed his family by not racing into his arms and screaming with joyful tears when he simply opened a box and pulled out a ring. No actual words were even spoken. He just waited for her to hold out her finger.

"Sierra?" Miranda's voice was stern.

"What?" Sierra replied with a down-turned expression and widened eyes of surprise.

"I've said your name three times. Are you on Mars?" Miranda said with exasperation.

"I didn't hear you. I---I guess I zoned out for a minute. I'm still tired from the trip. Even though I split the trip up and stayed in Charleston with a friend, I'm still exhausted. I think the nap I took made it worse. An hour of sleep was just enough to make me feel more dazed and confused than before," Sierra justified.

"I'm sure. We'll get going in a few minutes. I had made some barbecue yesterday for today's special since we were open later for the Pumpkin Patch Pow-Wow. I'm taking what's left home for us. There's plenty for all of us to eat tonight and leftover pumpkin mashed potatoes, as well. It may not sound like the perfect combination, but trust me. It's delicious," Miranda said. "The others will be a while getting back from the cabin. You can nap with Eden when we get home. That's if we can get the sugar rush to fade from that cake pop."

"What's the Pumpkin Patch Pow-Wow? I don't remember that," Sierra asked.

"This is the inaugural event. It's more or less an adult day at the pumpkin farm. Pumpkin ale and apple wine. Vendors from local stores were set up outside. Many ended up at the sports bar watching college football, it appears from the amount of leftover barbecue we have. I stopped by and bought a couple of wreaths and knick-knacks. I didn't partake in the beer party," Miranda said with mild sarcasm.

"I'm sure we'll appreciate the leftover barbecue. Their loss is our gain."

Sierra walked behind the bakery counter and lifted the handle of the plexiglass display case. She reached inside for a pumpkin spice coffee cake muffin, getting caramel syrup on her finger as she slid the muffin out. She admired it for a moment with its cinnamon and clove sprinkles adorning the drizzle of caramel syrup that swirled in the center. She tickled over her finger with her tongue as she delighted in the taste of sticky goodness.

It needs a dash of ginger and butter along the paper cups in the muffin pan next time. That would give a subtle spice and brown the bottom of the muffins for an unexpected final bite of flavor.

As the chime of the doorbell sounded, Sierra was brought out of her thoughts and alerted to a man of maybe 6 feet tall with hair that reminded her of hazelnut, and a thin beard surrounding a curved smile of curious acknowledgment. He began approaching the counter as Sierra stood motionless with crumbs on the corners of her mouth.

"Hey, there. I'd like a cup of coffee. Black. And, that muffin you're eating looks good. I'll take one of those, too," the man of Sierra's gaze said as he reached for a brown leather wallet from the back pocket of his jeans.

Sierra broke her silent stare. "Umm. We're closed. The register's already locked up. Sorry," she said with a shrug.

"I've been hearing about this place since I arrived in town last week. This is the first chance I've had to get by. The sign still says open. I'd really like to get a muffin. The crumbs on your lip make it quite enticing to try," he joked to sway her to serve him. "I've got cash. I can leave it for Monday morning. A pre-pay sort of thing."

Sierra wiped her mouth with a napkin and turned away as her cheeks pinked up.

"The coffee pot was turned off when I came in about ten minutes ago. I don't work here. I'm not even sure it's still hot, but if you're Okay with lukewarm or a microwave warm-up, I'll give you a cup," Sierra said, feeling her eyes narrowing with his persistence.

"I'd love some. Thank you kindly, ma'am. Although, I'm not sure the owners would be too happy about someone who doesn't work here hanging around behind the counter and eating their baked goods after closing. I'll keep your secret if you'll let me buy one of those muffins to go with the lukewarm coffee," he said with a wry smile and seafoam green eyes that reflected in the haze of the ever-popular 'golden hour' lighting pouring in from the cafe windows. "I'm Wes, by the way. Wes Carter."

Sierra twisted her lip around and brushed her hair over one shoulder. She walked over to the coffee pot and poured the medium-bodied brew into a paper cup. It was still fairly hot. Not piping, but enough to satisfy. She returned to the bakery case and removed a pumpkin spice muffin. As she set both on the counter, she placed her hands on her hips.

"You must be in sales, Mr. Carter. You don't strike me as someone who takes no for an answer very easily," she scoffed and then blinked her brown eyes, catching the rays of the peachy haze. The handsome newcomer surveyed Sierra's face. Her long golden hair. Her full cheeks and lips. The sparkle of her brown eyes. Her slim waist and bronzed skin.

"Not sales. I don't think I could sell cheese to mice. I'm a geologist. I dig in the dirt for a living. If I'm going to keep your secret of hanging out in diners and eating muffins, I'll need to know your name. Oh, and if you live in the area or just pass by diners and such as a wayward traveler surviving on late-day coffee and leftover baked goods," he said, stepping closer to the counter and taking a sip of the coffee.

"What do I owe you...Jane? Nah, you don't

look like a Jane. Mary? Nah. Help me out here."

Sierra shook her head and chuckled. "I'll give you the coffee. I'm not sure what the muffin is, but just give me three dollars. No worries about the owners coming after me. I know them pretty well. But next time, try to get in before five," she said. "If you're new in town, you should probably know that flirtation will get you far with some of the girls over at Frankie's Brewhaus across the street. Not so much here."

He handed Sierra a five-dollar bill. "Keep the change for your trouble. It's not a tip since you don't work here but for you just for putting up with me. I honestly have no *game*, but don't blame me for trying."

As Wes turned to walk away, Sierra contemplated stopping him. He had already opened the door when she decided to call out her name. "I'm Sierra."

As the door closed, Wes looked over as he walked by the cafe glass pane and nodded with a smile. Sierra rolled her eyes and smiled as their eyes searched each other for a moment.

She leaned against the bakery case and placed a loose fist over her mouth.

Miranda walked in with Eden. "Was there someone in here? Eden said she heard people talking. I was on the phone with your dad. He was making sure Tom was on the way to help him and Roxie move stuff out of the cabin and

Carlotta went out the back. Eden was in the office with me."

"Yes. A last-minute customer. Some new guy in town. Annoyingly persistent. I had to give in and let him have coffee and a muffin. I think he would've stayed for an hour pleading his case if I hadn't," Sierra said.

"Let's go before he comes back for a refill," she snarled with a chuckle that followed.

"Yes, we should get going. Your dad and siblings will be hungry after moving Roxie's mess. Honestly, I think a yard sale is in order for half of it," Miranda groaned as Eden tugged on her hand.

"Let's go, Nana!" Eden led her grandmother and aunt by the hands out of the cafe swinging her arms with theirs.

CHAPTER SIX

Family dinners at the Blake household had always consisted of overlapping conversations and college football on the television in the fall. Even now, with Sierra having lived half of the East Coast away, and Tom residing about fifteen miles outside of Mill Hollows, Saturday evening dinners in October were still mostly the same. The only differences are the addition of little Eden, and of course, the boiling pot of tension between Sierra and Roxie bubbling just beneath the proverbial lid.

"Pass the green beans, please," Tom said as he looked toward Roxie. She lifted the Blue Willow dish and tried to reach across the table to his left angle of her.

"Roxanne, you know we don't pass food that way in this house. Pass it to your sister across from you and she'll hand it to Tom," Richard ordered.

Sierra and Roxie glared at one another. Roxie rolled her eyes quickly and held the dish outward with a grimace. Sierra paused momentarily, entering into a stare-down of wills with her younger sibling, before taking hold of the stoneware bowl. The rest of the family dashed back into a conversation about cleaning the cabin and didn't notice their exchange.

"We've got to get a little tidying up done tomorrow before the tenant moves in later tomorrow evening. He's staying in a hotel in Blacksburg, but he's ready to get settled in," Richard said.

Sierra surveyed the table to see if she were the only one who seemed surprised by the news of a tenant moving into their family cabin Richard had built when she and her siblings were kids. It had been a hunting cabin and man cave of sorts until Tom was old enough to join in and then the two of them practically moved into it when Tom became a teenager. That was until, of course, Miranda put an end to overnight stays down the hill.

She had felt an emptiness when Sierra left for college and Roxie moved out of the house and into a camper park with her boyfriend a week after high school graduation.

"Who's moving into the cabin?" Sierra asked, leaning forward and cupping her hands in her lap below the mahogany table.

"A young man with a contract for the Corps of Engineers. He's doing something with rocks and sediment. I don't know. Something environmental down by the old gristmill. What's his name, Randa?" Richard asked with a fork in his hand twisting it in a circular motion and furrowing his thickened brows.

Miranda wiped her mouth delicately on both sides with her napkin. "Please lower your fork before you toss that green bean onto Roxie's lap, please," Miranda said flatly with a faint smirk.

A snicker floated around the room from everyone as Richard pretended he was going to poke Roxie's arm before obliging.

"Wes Carter is his name. Nice young man. Around the age of you girls. Roxie, he's cute, too," Miranda said with a smile and a tap on Roxie's hand.

"Mom, I'm not looking to meet anyone right now. Geez. I'm trying to get rid of one bum," Roxie groaned.

"Well, that's just it. It's time to meet someone who isn't a bum. Wes is a geologist. He's actually Dr. Wes Carter, I believe," Miranda added.

Sierra felt her pulse fasten. "Wait. Wes? I think that's the name of the guy who came into the cafe as we were leaving today. Does he have sandy brown hair and is about six feet tall?" Sierra inquired, noticing smiles around the table. Smiles from everyone except Roxie, who continued to eat her pumpkin mashed potatoes.

"I do believe that describes him pretty well. Did you happen to catch his eye color, as well, honey?" Miranda teased intrigued.

"No. (*Yes, I did. As green as fresh basil*). Of course not. I thought he looked a bit rough around the edges. I guess that explains it if he'd been digging in the dirt or whatever he's doing down there by the river and Dalton

Mill," Sierra said in an effort to sound uninterested.

"Maybe Sierra should go meet him when he arrives Monday. We have revival at church this week, and Roxie, you're going with Eden and me. It's not up for debate. You're staying with us, and it'll do you good to get out and see some people who love you," Miranda stated firmly. "Too much baggage for you over at the cabin. It's best if someone else deals with the tenant. Sierra, are you Okay with going over and making sure he gets his key and collect his deposit?"

"Sure. I guess I can handle that. I'm used to handing out keys and discussing rentals more than anyone else, so I'm quite certain I can handle getting him settled in," Sierra replied.

"Why does Sierra get to skip out on revival?" Roxie asked with a look of disdain. "She's living here too, at least for however long she's in town for."

"Sierra doesn't have a child to set an example for. You do. End of discussion." Miranda eyeballed Roxie as Eden began bouncing in her seat.

"Eden, baby. I'm sorry. Of course, I'll go to Revival with you and Grandma" Roxie said as her eyes welled with tears.

"I'll go Tuesday, so your mama can take a bubble bath. Can she borrow your rubber ducky?" Sierra asked, beaming at Eden as she fought back the thickening of emotion forming in her throat. Roxie softened her expression and breathed in deeply; pressing her lips into a curved unspoken sign of gratitude.

Everyone rose from the table and Roxie exited with Eden down the hallway avoiding eye contact with Sierra. Tom and Sierra cleared the dishes.

"Go on. I've got this. I know you're exhausted from helping at the cafe and then helping Dad and Roxie at the cabin," Sierra said.

"I hope you and Roxie can clear the air while you're home, sis," Tom said as he handed a glass to Sierra.

"Well, it certainly won't be for a lack of time. I'm staying for a while. I haven't told Mom and Dad yet, but I'm home for at least a month or two until I decide my next move. I've got my stuff being delivered in a few days from Florida to a storage unit in town. I had no idea Roxie would be moving in at the same time, however. I may need to come to stay with you."

"Let's not be too hasty," Tom chuckled. "I'm a total bachelor and I think you and Roxie will make amends faster if you're under the same roof."

Sierra nudged Tom's shoulder with her own. "Get outta here, little brother."

*****

Footsteps clambered down the hardwood floors of the hallway in a pitter-patter of enthusiasm. Eden rounded the corner into the kitchen with an old Cabbage Patch doll that had once belonged to Roxie snuggled in her arms. Sierra reminisced for a moment over an argument she'd had with Roxie over the doll as children. It had been at a yard sale when Amanda, the blonde-haired Cabbage Patch Kid, had been discovered by Sierra.

She had been around eight and Roxie around five. Roxie had blonde hair at the time, although it had later turned to the same dark blonde-caramel brown as Sierra's. She had wailed embarrassingly for the doll, insisting it looked like her and not Sierra. As usual, Sierra had given in and handed her younger sibling the doll. She was glad now that it had remained in good condition since Roxie played with it for a week or so until she got a bike for her birthday. Roxie was always more inclined to play in the mud, while running through sprinklers irrigating their family's tobacco crops than playing with dolls. Sierra had taken over the doll. She had slept with it next to her and even talked to it. She felt as though Amanda the Cabbage Patch Kid was the sister she preferred to Roxie.

"What is it, sweetie? Shouldn't you be getting ready for your bath and bedtime?"

Sierra asked kindly as she put the final dish into the cabinet.

"Milk. My night-night milk. Mama cwying. She said 'find Aunt Rie'," Eden said, rubbing her fingers over the doll's eyes as if she were wiping away tears.

Sierra felt a lump forming in her throat. "Sure, baby. Does Amanda need night-night milk?" Sierra asked, noticing a little doll bottle on the counter.

"Yes, pwease," Eden said as her cheeks filled and a smile displayed her dimples of joy only a child could possess.

After sitting with Eden and her doll for a few minutes, Sierra walked her down the hall and knocked on Roxie's door. Roxie opened it with reddened eyes and puffed lids. Her teal blue eyes usually sparkled like the Caribbean. Tonight, they were dull and showed signs of despair.

Roxie shifted her face quickly downward to Eden and turned on the cheering squad of happiness. "Come on baby. Let's go get you in the tub. Time for Mr. Ducky, so let's leave Amanda on the bed, Okay?"

Eden did as told and bounced across the room to take her mother's hand. Sierra followed them.

"I can give Eden her bath if you...you know, need some alone time," Sierra said softly.

"I've got it. Thanks. This isn't my first rodeo with feeling the weight of the world on my shoulders. My child always comes first, though," Roxie replied without looking back at Sierra.

As Roxie turned off the water and helped Eden inside, Sierra watched from the doorway. She was in awe of her sister's ability to shift gears from one emotion to the next so quickly. Inner strength was something both possessed when times were tough, but Roxie had far more obstacles than Sierra had encountered. Granted, many of Roxie's issues were by choices made at will, but still. Sierra watched Roxie splash water and play with the rubber duck as though she had just returned from a day at the beach rather than a day spent working, moving out belongings into her parents' home, and crying over the realization that she would have to explain why Eden's dad wouldn't be around anymore.

Sierra pulled the door closed behind her and paused. Her own life was in chaos. If ever there was a time to lean on each other, this was it. She needed her sister, and it was abundantly clear that she was needed in return.

Sierra breathed in deeply. She was not one to cry easily. She hadn't shed a tear when she ended her relationship with Miles, nor when she packed up her office without any job prospects. She had only shed tears in private when her mother had been diagnosed and battled cancer. Being the oldest child, she had always put on a brave face.

Roxie had accused her of being cold and

detached. Perhaps she was a bit detached if she were honest. It's how she dealt with remaining focused on the tasks at hand. It's why she had likely never given anyone her whole heart; always keeping a safe distance.

Standing on the other side of the door, listening to her sister exude false smiles to cover her pain, brought salt into Sierra's mouth and moistened lids around her eyes.

CHAPTER SEVEN

Morning dew glistened atop blades of grass as a dense fog ascended from a fishing pond in front of the Blake family's modest ranch-style brick home. Sierra sipped a rich dark brew coffee from a large mug as steam swarmed around the edges. She pulled the opening of a long beige cable-knit cardigan upon her bare shoulder, and secured her feet on the rail of the front porch, leaning back against the cushion covering a wooden patio chair. Her brown Ugg short boots warmed her feet. The chill of the crisp Autumn air wafted across her face, as she ran her finger around the rim of the coffee mug.

I've missed this. Fall weather. Changing leaves. Watching them tither to the ground.

Sierra surveyed the open view of the Virginia countryside she'd often taken for granted in the past. Rolling hills in the distance provided a wondrous backdrop for the rising sun. A family of deer scurried across the tree line of pines and into the woods behind them. She peered over at the cabin in the distance.

Wes Carter had arrived late the night before. She had seen headlights as they had turned down the drive. Living next door to her would be a handsome stranger she'd felt both annoyed by and attracted to upon their first meeting. She raised her brows and propped her hand against her cheek, leaning over to rest her head upon it. She noticed a silver Tundra parked in the driveway next to the cabin. Rising from the chair, her cardigan slid below her shoulder once again, exposing her black tank and leggings. She leaned against a post and took a sip of coffee.

Guess I'll be seeing you soon, Dr. Carter.

CHAPTER EIGHT

Richard appeared in the mudroom, groaning as he removed his soiled work boots. He began washing his hands in the sink as Sierra entered the kitchen and into his view.

"Sierra. Help me get this wet shirt over my head. I slipped in a dang puddle while walking back to my truck. I was about to take some firewood over to the cabin for the tenant."

Sierra tugged at the damp shirt and aided her father in removing it, all the while turning up her nose as she stood behind him. She had helped her dad many times when she was younger with removing dampened shirts from working in the fields when they had a tobacco farm. There was no sweat quite like that from a hard day's work in a tobacco field. She could still smell the leaves from the plants as the memory floated through her mind.

Richard meandered across the tiled floor of the kitchen as Sierra followed.

"Do you want me to take the firewood over?" Sierra asked, hoping the answer would be no, as she didn't envision her next encounter with the handsome stranger who was now living only footsteps away to be with firewood in her arms.

"No. I'm going to change into something dry and head over there. You could go on over for me and check the stove to make sure it works. Roxie failed to share that only one stove eye was working and that the oven wouldn't heat over 350. I had hoped that good-for-nothing live-in freeloader would have fixed it. That was his job, after all. He said he had his own handyman business doing home improvement and whatnot. Personally, I never heard of any real jobs he did and he certainly didn't fix anything at the cabin. Don't even get me started. I'm hoping she's done with him for the last time. He won't be welcome back on my property. That's for sure," Richard fumed.

"Get him to compile a list of what's not working and I'll be over in an hour. I need to fill our wood box first before your mother leaves me. She's been after me for two weeks to get the box filled before the first cold snap of the season hits and it's going to later in the week."

Sierra nodded. After taking a quick peek in the bathroom mirror, she decided to skip her makeup routine. She didn't want to look as though she cared what Wes Carter thought about her appearance, although she did brush through her hair and swept it into a freshly loosened ponytail, and added a clear shade of lip gloss. A gargle of mouthwash to mask the smell of coffee breath and she was on her way across the field.

It was a cool and crisp morning with leaves aglow. A perfect firestorm of reds, oranges, bold yellows, and deep hues of almost purple. The wondrous beauty of the mountains in the distance exuded a masterpiece of art that many only viewed in magazines and art galleries. This was her own backyard. At least it had been. Going for walks along the picturesque waters and palm breezes of Tampa was tranquil and calming for certain, but Autumn in the Virginia mountains was invigorating and even mystical at times.

   She arrived at the steps to the cabin and a wave of prickles of warmth ran through her body. She paused, recharging her focus, and knocked on the door. After a minute, she reached to knock again, as the door opened against her folded hand in mid-air. Wes stood in the doorway, shirtless, and with dampened hair. Quickly lowering her arm, Sierra forced a half-smile and looked away.

   "Hi," she stammered. "I'm not sure if you remember me, but..."

   Wes interrupted with a widening grin. "Of course, I remember you. The cafe girl whom I had to coax into selling me coffee."

   Sierra nudged her lip. "I wouldn't say *'coax'*. More like asked nicely," she replied feeling more confident.

   "Yes. Well, what can I do for you? I'm guessing you're one of the Blake's daughters since you were in the cafe yesterday and now at my doorstep at 9 am."

"I'm Sierra," she asserted.

"I thought that's what I heard as the door closed at the cafe Saturday. Nice to see you again, Sierra Blake. It is still Blake isn't it?" His brows raised with curiosity.

"Yes, it's still Blake. Anyway, I'm here to..." she paused. "You know, I can wait if you need to go finish getting dressed or come back later," she said, unnerved by his perfectly aligned abs and chest hair that lingered over his chiseled midsection.

Miles would never have opened the door without a shirt on. His chest would've been covered in baby oil and a Caribbean tan if he did. He was always slippery to the touch. Another sign he wasn't the one.

"Are you waiting for me to shut the door in your face over my lack of full attire?" Wes asked amused as he cracked a grin reminiscent of James Toby.

Wes lowered his head and eased back up staring into her eyes in such a way that felt like he could see every inch of her soul.

"No, of course not. I just didn't want to make you uncomfortable, but I can see that is a rather impossible task. You're quite unabashed about...well, you know," Sierra said. Her cheeks filled into a rosy pink upon realizing she was waving her hand over his torso.

*Why am I fumbling my lips over my teeth like
a teenager adjusting to new braces? What is
wrong with me?*

Wes pivoted, leaving the door ajar.
"Perhaps I should throw this on to make you
feel a bit more comfortable," Wes smirked as
he grabbed a flannel red and black cotton shirt
off of a chair. He motioned for Sierra to come
inside.

"Come in, please. The wind is kind of
howling this morning, isn't it?"

Sierra stepped inside the cabin and tucked
her hands into the pockets of her oversized
cardigan. Wes stepped closer to her; shirt still
partially unbuttoned. She swallowed hard and
straightened her back. Wes closed the door
behind her and slowly walked by her,
breathing out as he neared her neck. He was
enjoying watching her squirm.

"Anyway, Dad said for me to come by and
check the stove and get a list of anything not
working. He'll be over shortly to bring
firewood for the wood box," Sierra said,
feeling relief at finally mustering a string of
complete sentences without fidgeting. She
walked over to the kitchenette and began
twisting a knob on the stove to test the
burners.

A mostly buttoned-shirted-Wes leaned on
the countertop on the other side. "There's one
burner working, but really, that's all I need.
I'm going to replace the wires underneath that

run to the other three later today, though."

Sierra shut off the knob and turned to face Wes. "We can do that for you, or deduct from your rent for fixing it. I'm sure that's what Dad will say," Sierra replied.

"Nonsense. I like fixing things up when it's something I can fix, that is. My dad owns an appliance store and repair shop. I've never met a stove that I couldn't fix or use parts from. I'm going to fix the leaky faucet in the bathroom sink, also. It just needs a new washer, and tightening back up."

Sierra liked the idea of her parents having a tenant next door who would be a good neighbor to them, and a handyman to boot.

"Don't let Dad on to how Handy Andy you are or be forewarned; he'll be asking you to help him fix something on the tractor or mend a fence next."

They both chuckled. "If I didn't have so much work to do and were going to be here longer, I wouldn't mind. Although, I'm handy with more interior projects than farm equipment and such," Wes added.

"If you do think of anything, here's my cell. You can just shoot me a text. I'll let Dad know. He doesn't buy into texting and modern technology. While I'm here, I'll be happy to relay issues or assist if I can. How long do you think you'll be in Mill Hollows?" Sierra inquired.

Wes walked over to the refrigerator and took out two bottles of water. Would you like one?" Sierra smiled and accepted.

"I'm not sure exactly," Wes began. "My contract with the Corps of Engineers is for three months. I'm collecting soil samples and running lab tests to determine if there's any coal ash from a spill down in North Carolina that may have migrated, as well as other pollutants. The state wants to install a new water mill along the river and the county wants to turn an old flour mill into a historical landmark. Both require safety testing and regulations. Red tape type of stuff. Depending on how the process goes, I could leave earlier or have my contract extended. What about you? Your dad said you live in Tampa, right?"

"Yes. I'm a hotel manager. Well, I was. I'm taking some time off." As Sierra contemplated what to share and keep to herself, a knock at the door interrupted their conversation. Richard called out. "Hey, Wes. Sierra. You two in there?"

They replied for him to enter. Sierra moved toward the living room space as Wes greeted Richard.

"I got you some firewood. You wanna help me load it in the box?" Richard asked in a husky voice.

"I'm right behind you. I was getting acquainted with your lovely daughter. I was just asking how long she's in town for," Wes said, looking back at Sierra.

"I wish she'd move back up here. Florida has had her for a long time. That salty air and warm weather year-round are hard to beat with that one. She's always been part fish. You know, swim team, skiing, and suntans."

Sierra and Wes exchanged a silent shrug as Sierra rolled her eyes and smiled.

"I'm not sure, Dad. I'm kind of summered out these days. The appeal changes when you live in a tropical city for several years. You start to miss the seasons. I know I'm loving the weather since my arrival. I usually make it home for Christmas and in the summer. I've made more trips home while Mom was sick, but my only focus was on her during those visits. I finally feel like I can breathe and not be on a schedule. I'm not sure how long I'm staying, but I'm going to enjoy every moment while I am here."

"We're glad to have ya home for as long as we've got ya. Wes, too bad she's taken. She's a looker, ain't she?"

Wes nodded and ran his hand through his light brown hair, as it glistened in the sun shining along the porch. He cleared his throat, and widened his cheeks, as a mortified Sierra did her best to inch past both of the men in her path to the yard.

"Yes, sir. She is most certainly a beautiful woman. I'm sure someone in Florida is a lucky guy," Wes said as he reached the yard behind Sierra and Richard.

"I've got to get going. I'll see you later, Dad. Wes...I'm sure I'll see you around," she said flatly with a hastened glance of polite acknowledgment among the Halloween freak show that was happening at her expense.

Typical dad. Usually, mothers are known for matchmaking. Not in my family.

CHAPTER NINE

Roxie rushed into the cafe tying an apron around her waist over her jeans. She darted into the restroom and tossed her purse-slash-everything tote onto the counter and began swiftly applying a coat of foundation over her blotchy skin. Although most women of her twenty-six years of age could go sans makeup; late nights of tossing and turning while being kicked in the stomach, arms, and thighs by a three-year-old sleeping ninja didn't provide the necessary beauty sleep needed to hide darkened circles and puffiness.

She dabbed a lip gloss wand over her lips and rubbed them into a popping sound. She had been late getting Eden to preschool after a night of lying awake had led to snoozing the alarm for too long.

After a shrug and a frown in the mirror of the lesser version of herself staring back and judging her, Roxie grabbed her bag and headed into the kitchen.

"Sorry, Carlotta. I'm going to get it together soon. I promise. Well, I hope."

Carlotta rubbed Roxie's shoulder. "It's alright, Roxanne. You'll get through this. You're strong, like your mother."

Roxie smiled and began whisking eggs in a bowl.

Sierra entered from the front door and greeted neighbors and family friends as they dined. Roxie watched from the kitchen as her sister exuded confidence and enthusiasm as she twirled from one table to the next. She wished she had that congenial spirit. People had always gravitated toward Sierra.

Carlotta cleared her throat and nudged Roxie and raised her brow sternly.

"I think the eggs are ready for the quiche pan, don't you?"

Roxie looked down at the grip she still had on the whisk and removed it.

"Yes, I'd say so. I love my sister, Carlotta. You know I do. It's just...sometimes I feel like she has the ocean at her feet and I have nothing but mud at mine. I mean, moving to Tampa only made that feeling become more...what's the word? See, she'd know the word I'm looking for."

Sierra bounced in. "What word are you looking for?" A curious Sierra inquired as she overheard the end of the conversation.

Carlotta interjected. "A word for something being real. Like really happening instead of a joke about it happening."

Sierra wrinkled her brow. "Literal?"

"That's it. That's the word I was looking for. Told ya Sierra would know," Roxie said, pursing her lips.

Sierra contemplated asking about the topic

but chose to leave it be. She wasn't naive to her sister's envy. She was sure somehow in the five minutes since she'd entered the cafe, she'd managed to offend or fluster her sibling.

Miranda and Richard walked in a short time later and took a seat by their corner table with a view of the fall fruit and pumpkin stand next door.

Sierra and Roxie were doing their best dodge dances to avoid interaction more than necessary as Miranda stepped into the kitchen to check on the food supply and put in their order.

After doing everything but a white-gloved inspection, Miranda did a final taste test of the buttercream frosting Sierra had whipped up from scratch.

"This is divine, Sierra. This is for the cupcakes for the afternoon?"

"Yes. I meant to come in earlier, but Dad had me go over and check on Wes; I mean the tenant," Sierra abruptly corrected. She placed a fallen tendril of hair behind her ear and returned to the frosting station she had set up.

"Roxie, how's the quiche coming along? Will they be ready for lunch?" Miranda asked. She tasted a sample Roxie handed her on a plate.

"Yum. Butternut squash, pimento cheese, and bacon. I taste a hint of sweetness. Is that hazelnut?"

"Yes. Carlotta suggested it. Just a teaspoon mixed in," Roxie replied as Sierra and Carlotta exchanged looks of a lifelong secret pact between accomplices of a crime. Roxie would never have agreed to add the hazelnut had she known it was actually Sierra's suggestion.

"You've got a knack for quiche, dear. Omelets too. Speaking of omelets, whip one up for your dad. He wants an omelet with ham, peppers, and onions. I, on the other hand, am ready to devour this slice of quiche."

"I'm glad you approve, Mom," Roxie said with a mix of pride and boredom, as cooking was not something that gave her the joy it seemed to give Miranda and Sierra.

"So, mom. Roxie. There's something I need to tell you all. It'll only take a minute," Sierra said with a bit of shakiness in her voice; hair twirling around her finger in an attempt to calm her nerves. Miranda motioned to Richard to join them in the kitchen.

"I think it's best if I rip the band-aid off rather than opening up a Q and A session over it. So, here goes." Sierra blew out her cheeks and began to speak with more composure.

"I broke up with Miles. Well, he proposed in front of everyone in the company and humiliated me, but that's beside the point. I didn't want to marry him. It didn't feel....right...it just didn't. After that, he basically blackballed me from the resort with an offer of relocation that he knew I wouldn't accept. So, there it is. Your oldest daughter is home. Unemployed. Unmarried. And....feeling terrified and liberated at the same time. Please no questions about it. All that matters is that I am going to find a job soon. I have savings and will not be a burden on you. I just need a little time to figure out my next step."

Everyone can pick their jaws up from the floor at any time.

Miranda and Richard exchanged blank stares. Richard nodded.

"Well, alright then. You know you're always welcome home with us. Maybe if you stick around here for a while, you'll decide to stay. In Mill Hollows, that is. We're hoping to get both of you girls out of the house sometime soon. I don't know if there are enough walls for both of you to stay under the same roof for too long."

Sierra and Roxie shifted looks toward each other and back to their parents.

"You girls can both work here in the meantime, then. That's settled," Miranda said with a firmness that everyone knew not to question. Sierra and Roxie nodded in agreement.

CHAPTER TEN

As the lunch rush at the Salted Caramel Cafe tapered off, Sierra noticed Roxie had disappeared from the kitchen. She leaned into the kitchen and motioned toward Carlotta.

"Where's Roxie?"

"She stepped outside to take a phone call. Someone has been calling and texting her all morning. I'm afraid it's Toby," Carlotta said with concerned eyes.

Sierra felt her body shift into protective older sister mode with a swiftness that only her family could bring out in her otherwise, mostly cool-headed demeanor. She stepped outside in the back of the cafe to hear Roxie raising her voice as she sat with her head down and rocked her knee on a nearby picnic table. She moved closer to listen in.

'Why have you put me in this position? Now, you're going to jail, and can't even pay any child support for your daughter! It wasn't like you were much help before, but now...what am I supposed to tell Eden? I don't want her knowing her daddy is in jail.'

Sierra folded her arms and leaned against

the brick. She hadn't realized how much her sister was really going through.

'We're done, Toby! I'm not paying to get you out this time. I don't know what I'm telling Eden, but one thing I do know. She deserves better and now I finally see that I do too. Just do your time, get some help, and maybe...just maybe you'll get to see your child again. But not now. You need help, Toby.'

Roxie tossed her phone into the grass and placed her hands behind her on the table. Sierra rushed over and sat beside her. Sierra rubbed her sister's back as they sat in silence for the next few minutes.

"Roxie, what can I do? What do you need from me? I'll help you get through this."

"There's nothing anyone can do, Sierra. It's my fault. I should have let him go to jail the last time he was caught with marijuana in the car. I have always tried to support him. He's the father of my child. Ya know? But, I'm just tired. I am over it all. I'm tired of the cafe. I'm tired of feeling miserable. The only bright spot in my life is Eden."

"Well, I'm here now. I know we have our issues, but you need me. Take the rest of the week off from the cafe. I'll help Carlotta. I'll talk to Mom. She's doing so well now. She can come in and help more. She probably wants to, but doesn't want to be in your way."

They exchanged looks and chuckled.

"Well. We know that's not our mom's concern, but I really do think she's trying in her own way to let you take charge because she thinks this is what you want. I know that it's not. You've always let Mom think you enjoyed cooking and working here, but you don't do you?"

"I don't hate it. I just don't love it the way you did growing up. I enjoyed being a hairstylist. When Mom got sick, I had to step in. Someone had to."

"You're right. You've been the one here to make sacrifices when I couldn't. I mean, I could have. Perhaps I should have," Sierra said as a pang of guilt consumed her.

"No. Don't do that. I resent you on the one hand, but I admire you on the other. You're the one with the education and personality to run a business. I know you were happy at the resort. I just assumed you had it all. The perfect life that I'd never have. I'm almost happy you lost your job. I'm sorry. I'm a terrible sister."

"No, you're not. You just have a hard time stepping into someone else's shoes. I can see how hard it is for you to do that with all that you have dealt with, though. Come on. Let's go inside. Have a pumpkin spice latte and that leftover plate of cheddar biscuits Carlotta has hidden in the warmer. Then, go home. I'll go get Eden from preschool. I'll go to revival tonight and you just rest."

"No. I'll go to Revival. I think I need Jesus more than ever right now. You go see that handsome new neighbor. I've seen him. He stopped by to check out the cabin last week."

"Let's go, sis. We've got this, I promise," Sierra said as she squeezed Roxie's shoulder with her arm.

CHAPTER ELEVEN

Sierra returned from the cafe to find Miranda and Eden in the kitchen having a milk nightcap. She found Roxie curled up on the couch asleep. Sound asleep. The kind of sleep that sends one into another dimension and leads to drooling emissions. Miranda placed a plush blanket over Roxie as Eden giggled at hearing her mother snore.

"Come now, sweet pea. Let's not wake your mama," Miranda whispered as she took Eden by the hand and led her down the hall. Sierra brushed her sister's hair away from her face gently, remembering how many times she'd shoved her foot against Roxie when they were teenagers and Roxie would begin to snore in the middle of a movie. She would always insist upon staying up late to watch a movie with Sierra but rarely made it through a full viewing before drifting into sleep. It had annoyed her then, but now it made her long for those simpler times.

Sierra quietly walked down the hallway and into Roxie's room. "I'll give Eden her bath. I told Roxie I'd do it," Sierra said.

"I'll do it. Grandma hasn't bathed this one since they moved in," Miranda said as she tickled Eden's waist. "You just relax. Roxie isn't the only one in need of a little self-care time. I let her skip the revival service tonight, as she was sleeping like a baby when we got home."

Sierra heeded her mother's advice and changed into fleece leggings and an old Virginia Tech sweatshirt she'd found in her closet. She pulled her hair into a ponytail and slid into her suede boots.
As she stepped outside onto the side steps from the mudroom, Richard shut off his old Ford pickup truck and met her in the yard.

"Where ya headed?"

"I'm going for a walk down the driveway or something. Roxie's getting some much-needed sleep on the couch, so we're giving her a little longer before waking her."

"I'm glad. I don't think she's been getting much sleep lately. I'll take my boots off after I ease in the door and head on back to the den. I had my monthly Lodge meeting and am stuffed. I can't wait to get in my *jammies* as Eden calls them. You should be careful out here. Darkness and mountain life don't mix for walking around."

"I know. I need my bat I used to carry around when I was younger. I may just sit on the front porch or the back deck. Breathe in the fresh mountain air."

"Now that sounds strange coming from a girl who couldn't wait to have summer all year long in Florida."

"I still like my summer weather, but I'm not missing Tampa like I thought I would. At first, I thought I'd apply to other resorts in Miami and perhaps Ft. Lauderdale or The Keys. It truly is beautiful there. I wish you had visited with Mom. Roxie too. Mom and Tom are the only two I could pry away from Mill Hollows."

"I'm sorry, honey. You know it would take a life-or-death situation to get me on an airplane. Roxie must have inherited my fear of flying and attachment to country life. Neither of us like the beach either. I do hate we didn't visit you, though. I'll tell ya a secret. I'm glad you aren't marrying Miles. I was already dreading a tropical wedding since you worked at a resort. Can you see your old man dressed like Don Johnson from Miami Vice?"

They both snickered.

"Well, glad I kept you from having to get a spray tan, Dad."

****

Sierra rounded the corner toward the front porch when she spotted headlights going down toward the cabin. A moment later, she heard a door shut as it echoed over the pond.

Wes is home.

A jolt of excitement rushed over her as she contemplated going over to the cabin to say hello.

It would be nice to check in on our tenant. He did just move in. Of course, I was there this morning. If I go over, he'll think I'm some kind of stalker popping up out of the dark like a serial killer.

She found a seat on the top step and tucked her knees inward, placing her feet on the step below. A few minutes later, she heard a door shut again and headlights illuminating the driveway from the cabin toward the road. She watched as the truck turned onto the road and then, surprisingly, into her driveway.

He's coming over here.

It was too late to rush into the house. He'd see her. The headlights of the Toyota were now picking her up in the edge of their glow. Quickly, they went dark.

"Hey, Sierra. Sorry about the lights. I didn't mean to blind ya. I wasn't expecting anyone to be outside, but then again, it's a great night to sit outside. You're just missing a fire pit," Wes said as he approached the bottom step, bag in hand.

"I think it's going to be colder starting tomorrow. A fire pit would be a great idea for sure," Sierra replied.

"So, is your boyfriend joining you since you're here for a while?" Wes asked, rocking on his heels.

"Umm. No. My dad didn't know at the cabin this morning, but I dropped that fun little bomb at the cafe. I ended things with my ex, Miles, before coming home. Suffice to say, he will not be joining me."

"I'm sorry. I hope you're Okay." A mix of pleasure and concern fought for his attention.

"I'm fine. He wasn't the one. He wanted to get married and I knew he wasn't who I envisioned myself growing old with. Really, I'd rather move forward."

"Okay. I won't pry any further. I wanted to drop off some mail for your sister that was in the mailbox. I don't know if she's checked it in a few days, but there was a bunch of stuff in there. I put it all in this bag. Most of it is probably junk, but anyway. I'll give it to you."

Sierra took the bag as their hands touched in the exchange. Even in the dusk of darkness, they caught each other's stare for a moment; each softly curving their lips upward.

"Guess I'll leave ya to your porch meditation session, then." Wes' lips opened into a crooked smile as he rubbed his hand over his scruffed face.

"Yeah, Okay. Do you have everything you need...I mean, in the cabin?" Sierra said as she leaned back on her hands, hoping to sound aloof.

"I don't know if I have *everything* I need, but I definitely think I'm going to like living here for a while. Your family are top-notch landlords. You know," Wes said as he turned clockwise away from Sierra and paused. "I'm off tomorrow, and I'd like some company on a canoe ride down the Roanoke River if you'd like to tag along. If it's not your kind of thing, that's cool," he said, returning to face her as he fidgeted with his hands in his back pockets.

Sierra had loved canoeing when she was younger. She hadn't been in a few years. She leaned against the porch column and tilted her head.

"Sure. That sounds fun. I haven't been canoeing in a long time."

"Great. I'll pick you up at about 10?"

"See ya then," Sierra replied, biting her lip.

As Wes drove away, Sierra watched him until she heard the sound of the truck door closing once more across the way. She stretched her arms out and spun around.

He makes my heart pound and my head spin. I've never felt this way for someone I haven't even dated. Truthfully, I've never felt this way...ever.

CHAPTER TWELVE

An adrenaline-inducing force of chilled air tumbled down from the mountain peaks upon the lower elevation of Mill Hollows. The sway of tree branches cast leaves into the air; floundering and frolicking toward the ground. Sierra closed her window as Wes turned into the driveway; an olive green shaded canoe was visible from the truck.

Sierra wrapped a knitted infinity scarf around her neck. She had convinced Roxie to braid her hair into French braids down each side. She slipped into her old hiking boots she had found tucked away in the closet.

Thank goodness I kept these old boots. If I decide to stick around, I think investing in new ones will be a necessary purchase.

Wes knocked at the side door as Sierra hurriedly grabbed a puffy North Face vest from the back of her closet. She never needed the coat in Florida, so she was thankful for the quick access to warmer attire than her bags contained.

Growing up in the Roanoke Valley had taught her how rapidly weather patterns can change in the mountains. It was one of the reasons she had chosen to move to Florida, as she assumed she'd deal with warm weather consistently. She hadn't considered that even in beautiful Tampa, it could rain and return to blue skies at any moment on repeat each day.

"Hi," Sierra said with a higher pitch than usual. "I'm all set," she added, forcing her decibel level down from *'winning a million dollars to a normal day on the lake'* volume.

"Hey, yourself. I...umm...like the braids. Very Eddie Bauer," Wes said as his pulse began to race. He continued standing in the doorway.

Noticing his appreciation of her appearance pleased Sierra and comforted her anxiousness.

"I'm ready when you are," Sierra said with a confident grin and a shrug.

"Yeah, umm. Not sure why I'm blocking your exit. Let's do this," Wes replied, pivoting on his heel and giving himself an inner scolding.

"Man, pull yourself together."

****

A ride through the winding roads of rural farmland and mountain views seemed different than all the times before as Sierra breathed in the contentment of her surroundings. Sitting close to a man in perfectly fitting jeans, a sun-kissed golden glow upon his face, and one hand hung over the steering wheel, made the journey to Carvin's Cove an excursion all its own.

If we turned around and drove back right now, my day would be complete.

Sierra was not alone in her thoughts, as Wes was already devising a plan to drive left-handed on the way back, in hopes of adjoining his right one with Sierra's left if the day went well.

Dating hadn't been on Wes Carter's radar in quite some time. Traveling as a geologist had taken him all over the Midwest for the past few years. He never stayed in one place long enough to form any attachments to anyone, despite being sought after as the new guy in a few other small towns along the way.

"Do you mind if we make a stop here," Wes said as they neared the red-covered bridge leading them out of Mill Hollows. He pulled over to a graveled lot.

"I used to love coming out to the trails here growing up," Sierra said. "This is the most photographed spot in Mill Hollows and for miles beyond. My mom calls it the Bridge of Madison County, in reference to a Clint Eastwood and Meryl Streep film."

Wes chuckled. "I've heard of it. I'm sure my mom watched it, as well. This is where I'm doing my work. It's beautiful out here. I've watched a family of deer crossing the creeks every morning. I saw a black bear the other day. He was eating berries that had fallen onto the ground from a bush."

They walked down toward a large rock with the bridge in full view from behind. Wes pulled out his cell phone and took a photo of the bridge. They watched as a woman took a selfie on a rock. They walked over to her and Wes offered to take a photo for her. She thanked him.

"You two look so in love," the woman said, as Wes and Sierra exchanged devious smiles of amusement. "I remember those days of young love. I lost my husband last year. We used to drive out here every Autumn and visit the bridge and go walking along the trail by the old mill."

As tears welled in her eyes, Sierra touched her shoulder and pulled her in for a gentle hug. They nodded in agreement not to correct her assumption. Secretly, both wanted what she described.

"Now, you two get over there and let me take a photo for you," the woman demanded.

Sierra and Wes exchanged hesitant looks, waiting on the other to make the first move to get into a faux couple model pose.

"Now, the stiff pose is over. Let loose. Dip her or something."

Wes was eager to oblige as infectious laughter took over from nervous awkward waist and shoulder touches. He pulled Sierra closer to him. It was the first time both had felt a longing to kiss the other and an inability to move away. The woman took a photo and smiled with glee.

"Now, dip," she ordered.

Wes leaned over Sierra as he scooped her back into his arms, lowering her into his grasp. The woman moved around them and continued to click the phone's camera button. Sierra and Wes remained fixated on each other as he forcefully pulled her upward. She stumbled over onto him, placing her hands on his chest as he supported her waist.

"I got some cute shots," the lady said with pride.

Awaking from the momentary alternate universe they seemed to have escaped to, they promptly stepped aside and thanked the woman.

"Sorry about that. I didn't have the heart to tell her we weren't a couple," Sierra said.

"Neither did I," Wes replied. "I'm not complaining about holding a beautiful woman close for a few photos. I'm up for impromptu photos with you anytime," he chuckled.

"Come on. Let's take a short walk near the mill." Wes motioned for Sierra to follow him down toward a small flowing creek. He reached his hand to assist her down a rocky hill.

"I can handle myself," Sierra said playfully. Upon taking her next step, her foot slid and Wes caught her as she toppled over a rock wedged deep into the ground.

"You were saying?" Wes mocked, still holding onto her arms against his chest.

"Don't blame me. Blame that rock that didn't move for my feet," Sierra scoffed.

"I'm calculating sediment and land shifts along the trails. Collecting soil samples for environmental testing."

"A three-month contract. That's what you said at the cabin, right? Are all of your contracts short-term?"

"Yeah. I don't spend much time in one place. I haven't been in one state longer than six months since getting my doctorate a few years back. I was lucky that I was able to finish school with my master's degree and then work in Colorado while getting my doctorate. That's where my hometown is. Greeley."

"I love Colorado," Sierra added. "I went on a ski trip once in college and again a few years ago to Aspen. I'd love to see other parts of the state when it isn't covered in snow. I imagine it's breathtaking and our mountains are quite different."

"There's good and bad to anywhere you live. I miss Colorado, but I don't miss the winters. It would already be snowing by now back home. I'm enjoying getting to savor Autumn for a bit. Even a few days of lingering summer find their way up the mountain into late September from what I've been told. I like Virginia so far. It's growing on me rather quickly."

"Do you think there's any chance you could settle down and call somewhere home soon or is life on the road what calls out to you?"

"That's a good question. Two years ago, I'd have answered that much faster than I can now. When you move around, you don't have time to worry about much. It's exhilarating. But, it's also..."

"Lonely?" Sierra interjected as Wes paused and looked away. A wave of somber stillness grew over him.

"Yep. You learn to live with the fact that your friends get married and have kids. They say they're jealous of you, but really they aren't. They would trade places for a few weeks perhaps. It's just the way it is. I make good money and enjoy what I do, but now that I've spent so much time out of a suitcase, I'd like to find a more permanent position. I don't mind traveling occasionally, but staying in the cabin makes me want a home of my own. I'm usually in apartments or hotels. Occasionally, a house, but there's something about cabin living with a view of a mountain outside that's pretty hard to beat."

Sierra could relate to loneliness. Despite her relationship with Miles, she had felt alone for most of the time she'd been in Tampa. Friends came and went as life changed for them. Miles was really more of a friend who had pushed for more. That relationship had grown more from the want of someone special than palm-sweating, phone-checking, and butterfly-fluttering feelings of actually falling in love.

They arrived within view of Dalton Mill; an old flour mill that had been out of use for longer than Sierra's lifetime, but was still in good condition overall. The rock and wood exterior of the two-story building had been kept up in the past, but now needed repairs. A red wheel that once churned lies silently against the side.

"If the mill were more visible to those traveling by, this would be the hidden gem everyone would want as their photographic backdrop.

"When I was in high school, my friends and I would camp in the park nearby and we'd come here and hike the trails, pan mine, and of course, sneak cheap wines with us in our backpacks."

"Sounds like the kind of weekends we had in Colorado. I wonder if we would've hit it off if we'd met in high school. I doubt it. You would've thought I was a total science nerd. And you would've been accurate." Wes chuckled, reaching in front of them to push back a lowered tree branch. "If my rock jokes didn't win you over, my obsession with old muscle cars and loud exhaust pipes would have done the trick."

Sierra leaned onto his shoulder and pushed

back with a charmed laugh. "I'm not sure we would've been friends back then. I was a skater girl until my senior year. Converse shoes. Lots of black. So much so that my parents became concerned that I had joined a cult. I played my Avril Lavigne CD so often that my sister broke it in half in one of our many arguments."

Wes wrapped his arm around her shoulder and she took his hand as they made their way back up toward the truck.

"A skater girl and a rock collector. We would've been awesomely bad together," Wes said as he opened the door for Sierra to hop inside the truck. He shut the door and looked back at Sierra as he walked around to the driver's side.

CHAPTER THIRTEEN

Canoeing alongside nature's views brought serenity to those paddling Carvin's Cove; evident by the exuberant hand waves of passers-by. Kayaks and canoes traveled the water. Hikers in boots canvassed the trails along the embankment. Sunshine dazzled across the lake in a light show of sparkled glitter.

A woodpecker could be heard in the distance tapping along a tree. Scurries of squirrels and rabbits echoed from the brush-filled trees.

"This has been so much fun," Sierra said as they paddled toward the embankment. "I do see dark skies above, though. Virginia mountain weather. It changes without warning."

"I'm used to that in Colorado. Looks like we're heading in at the right time."

Droplets of rain began trickling from the trees overhead as they secured the canoe. With an agreeable chuckle, Sierra and Wes gave each other thumbs-up gestures and dashed into the truck as the rain pellets quickened against the windshield.

"At least the rain didn't catch us downstream about thirty minutes ago," Sierra said, buckling her seat belt.

"What's a little rain? I find it soothing. Purifying to the earth. Guess that's what happens when you spend your days digging in the soil and being prepared for all types of weather conditions," Wes added.

Sierra turned her head toward Wes. "I agree. I love snow for the same reason. I know it's messy when it melts, but it's beautiful when it covers the ground. I haven't seen snow in a few years now. I seem to miss it by a week or two during Christmas when I visit. I was here in the early spring and it snowed five inches the day after I left for Tampa."

"I'm actually kind of stoked about seeing it snow while staying at your family's cabin. I hope I get to see a snowfall while I'm here."

A knot formed in his stomach. He wasn't sure what it was about Sierra and Mill Hollows that made this assignment different from the others, but it was. After only a week in the sleepy mountain town, it was beginning to feel like a place he could call *home*. Sierra was part of that feeling. Being with her was easy and as soothing as the rain falling gently around them. He took a risk and reached for her hand.

Sierra slid her palm closer to his; a peace she hadn't known in longer than she could recall spilled over her body. Hand in hand, they listened to the rain without music or speaking. Being in the moment with each other spoke volumes over silence, as they drove down the country roads of the Roanoke Valley.

CHAPTER FOURTEEN

Roxie was pacing in the yard as Wes and Sierra came up the driveway. It was nearing time for her to go pick up Eden from preschool.

"I'd better go see what's going on with my sister. She's having a hard time with her ex; Eden's dad, right now."

Wes lifted her hand to his lips and kissed it. "This will have to do, then. I don't want to leave without letting you know how much fun I had with you today. Is there anything I can do for you or your sister? Someone's backside I need to kick?"

"No. That's a battle she's got to fight legally now. He's made his choices and they've led to him not being with his child and my sister. She's given him many chances. We have our issues, but I'm determined to help her get through this. I think she goes back because she doesn't want to burden Mom and Dad. This time, she's moved into the house and that's a huge step in the right direction. Toby knows how he will be greeted at the door if he shows up here and at my dad's home. I hope he gets help. Either way, he needs to be out of my sister's life and for now, Eden's, as well."

"I'm here if you need me. Anything. Anytime. Just know that. I'd love to have you over tonight. I think the cold weather followed that rain shower on the way in. It feels cooler than it did early this morning. How about that fire pit idea and steaks or chicken on the grill? I'm no chef, but I can handle a grill." His green eyes pleaded for an agreeable response.

"Sure. I'll bring a side dish and a dessert from the cafe. I'm sure there's something left over from today. I made five trays of spice cupcakes with buttercream frosting yesterday. I may or may not have brought home a container of a dozen last night," Sierra said as she pursed her lips and lifted her finger to her mouth.

Wes gave a wide grin. "Then, it's a date. I mean, it's just hanging out. Not really a date-date...unless, you know, you're cool with calling it that. You bring the stolen cupcakes and whatever you want. I'm not picky. I'll fix chicken and steak. Sound good?"

Sierra nodded. She blew out her cheeks as she turned to see Roxie head inside. "I'd better go check on her. Text me later and I'll see you tonight. Oh, and I'm good with calling it a date," she whispered as she leaned in and kissed his cheek.

CHAPTER FIFTEEN

Sierra was mentally preparing for yet another round of bad news plaguing her sibling. She had heard her sobs at night and prayed for comfort and good news. Feeling helpless was not acceptable in the Blake family.

"Hey, Rox," Sierra said softly as she touched her sister's shoulder from behind the couch. "Do you want to talk?"

Roxie reached up for her sister's hand. "It's good news, I guess. I'm just having a hard time processing everything. That was my lawyer. Toby's court hearing was today. I almost caved and went to the courthouse. I could have. I could have bailed him out once more and picked up shifts again at the sports bar or the Rusty Nail, heaven forbid. Whatever it takes is what I've done for our family. Not this time. I didn't go. I didn't let him pull me in and make me feel sorry for him. No more playing me like a fiddle because of Eden. I'm letting him stay in jail for himself and our child. Nothing will change if he doesn't suffer consequences for his actions. That's the bottom line. It's just..."

Sierra stepped around the couch and sat down beside Roxie. She leaned Roxie onto her lap and stroked her hair.

"I know. It's hard. It sucks. But..Rox, you're doing the right thing. I promise you. Whatever he does after this, do not let him come back into your life. That's a promise I need you to make to me and yourself. A promise for Eden. Maybe someday, he can sober up and see her as he proves himself worthy, but for now, he's got to want to sober up. Eden is his excuse. Saying he needs to have you and Eden in his life to stay sober. It hasn't worked so far. It isn't going to. He has to get help and starting with his jail sentence is where it has to be."

Roxie wiped away tears. "You're right. This is it. One last cry. Tomorrow, Roxie-new and improved-begins."

CHAPTER SIXTEEN

Smoke from the grill was sending flavors of wood chips, mesquite, and seasonings floating through the evening air as Sierra arrived at the cabin. Wes was flipping steaks and chicken as she approached the patio.

"Smells good," Sierra said as she neared Wes.

"Let me help you with that," Wes said promptly as he removed two containers from her hands and carried them into the kitchenette. Sierra followed.

"You fixed that broken cabinet door. That was the first thing I noticed when I walked in the other day but didn't want to point out things in need of repair to a tenant out of the gate."

"Yes, I fixed that last night. I took care of the stove, also. So far, everything else seems to be working well. I love this place."

Sierra opened the containers. I brought over the cupcakes I mentioned, and we had some leftover pasta salad. I added some chopped walnuts and bacon bits to it. It gives it a little seasonal flair."

Wes reached for a fork and completed his own taste test. "Delicious. I hope my chicken and steak can match up."

Sierra ran her finger over a cupcake and touched Wes' nose with frosting. "That's how we begin taste tests for frosting in the Blake family," she said and burst into laughter.

Wes pulled her into him, catching her by surprise. He smeared frosting on her nose as he leaned his face against hers; kissing her passionately. As he released her, he ran his finger over her nose; wiping the smeared frosting onto his finger. He placed the edge of his finger in his mouth. "Yep. Taste test approved. Buttercream frosting for the win."

Sierra followed his lead and wiped frosting from his nose. "Agreed."

"I should get back out to the grill before I burn the entrees," Wes said.

Sierra paused for a moment, soaking in the unexpected kiss. She thought sure she'd know when that moment was about to happen. She'd always known when someone was about to kiss her for the first time. That included times she had ducked or turned away. She touched her lips. That moment. That kiss. She was falling in love with Wes Carter. How was it possible when she'd never been one to give her heart freely?

I hope this isn't what happens when one turns down a proposal. Falling head over heels for the first man one meets afterward. I want this to be real. Even if it is, he's only here for a few months. What if this is what he does? Leaves a trail of broken hearts along the banks of the rivers he encounters along the way. Maybe I deserve to have my heart broken for hurting Miles. But wouldn't it have hurt him far more if I'd stayed and accepted his proposal knowing he wasn't the one?

Wes returned to the doorway. "You coming out here? I've got a bottle of white and a bottle of red on the table if interested in a glass of wine. I'm having a shot of whiskey to fend off this cold shot of old man Winter happening tonight. I don't really drink. Socially now and then is about all. I figured you're likely a wine girl. Am I right?"

"I am typically a rum and pineapple juice girl. Like you, I don't drink often enough to have a real preference. I do enjoy a glass of wine now and again."

Wes entered and approached the table. "Pinot Grigio or Merlot? Does either strike your fancy, miss? Keep in mind, both are grocery store lower-end brands."

Sierra snickered and reached for a glass. "Let's go with the Merlot. It pairs better with the steak. I'm going to go with steak instead of chicken."

"Now, you're talking. Chicken is good, but nothing beats a good steak now and again. Come tell me how you like yours cooked."

How do I like it? Hmm. Hot. Sexy.

Wearing a thermal long-sleeved shirt and faded denim... Oh, he means the steak.

Sierra sipped wine and looked up at the stars, surveying the full moon lighting up the darkness. She could see her breath in the cold air.

"It's definitely feeling more like late Autumn tonight. Winter, even. I'm not ready for it to be this cold yet," Sierra said.

Wes turned off the grill and stepped toward her from behind. He wrapped his arms around her waist. She placed her arms over his as he leaned closer. She could feel his warm breath against her neck.

"Days like today and nights like this would be easy to get used to," Wes said softly.

"You've only been here less than two weeks. What happens when you or I have to go? Wes, is this...normal for you? I mean, do you meet women in towns where you work and it's all great for a while until...well until it's time to move on to the next geological contract."

Wes spun her around. "What? Of course not. I've made it a point not to date in most places I've been for that very reason. Sure, I'm human. I've dated, but it was always casual. For me. For them. But with you. Nothing about this is *normal.* Being with you. Being in Mill Hollows. It's everything. This cabin- that covered bridge-all of it. I'm falling in love with every part of this experience. Most of all, though, I'm falling in love with *you,* Sierra

Blake.

Sierra wrapped her arms tightly around Wes' neck as their lips met.

"I'm falling in love with you, too," she whispered into his ear.

"Look. I don't know what's going to happen after my contract. You don't know what your next move is either. What I do know is I want to figure out a way to be together. It's crazy, I know. But knowing you feel the same cosmic dance of emotions as I do so quickly can only mean this is real. That's what I know. Critics say people can't fall in love in a few days. If that were true, there wouldn't be a cliché of love at first sight. I'm not saying it was necessarily love the first time I laid eyes on those gorgeous cinnamon eyes or saw that crinkle in your nose when I coaxed you into serving me coffee, but something was happening, for me, at least, then and there in the cafe."

Sierra bit her lip. "You did have a certain charm about you, I guess. I liked your smile. It's disarming and curves up a little on one side."

"Really. That's all you've got after I just poured my heart out," he teased.

"Okay. I felt my pulse race when I saw you pull into the driveway of the cabin the night you moved in. Honestly, it's been racing every time I've seen you. I felt it even when I heard your name mentioned at my family's dinner table."

"That's more like it. Now, we'll figure out what to do about *later on* when *later on* arrives. For now, let's enjoy our dinner before it gets cold."

****

Wes brought in wood and placed it into the fireplace. He knelt and added starter sticks to get a fire going. Sierra watched him as she leaned against the counter with a glass of wine in hand.

"Need a hand?" she asked with a chuckle.

"I've got it. You can't rush a good thing. It takes time for the spark to catch and turn into more," Wes said as the logs began to glow from the rise of building flames. He raised onto his feet and spread his arms open; a smug grin of satisfaction perched over his lightly bearded jawline.

Sierra clapped her hands softly and made her way toward him. Wes slid her hair behind her shoulder on one side and kissed her neck.

"So, what was that about not rushing a good thing?" Sierra asked playfully.

"I'm not rushing anything. I'm taking all the time in the world," Wes said in a rasped softness as his lips found hers.   Embraced in each other's arms, time fell still.

CHAPTER SEVENTEEN

A FEW WEEKS LATER

A mermaid of just under three feet tall
entered the living room; plastic orange
pumpkin-shaped bucket in hand. Spiral
pigtails bounced around as Eden sashayed
around the room. Halloween hadn't been
celebrated in many moons inside the Blake
home since all of their children had grown up
and Eden was the only grandchild. This was
the first year Roxie was going to take her
trick-or-treating at the community center.

"Now, Roxanne. Don't let that child get a
bunch of candy and come home with a sugar
rush before bedtime," Richard warned. Eden
jumped between his knees and he tickled her
sides. Giggles filled the air. Miranda entered
from the hallway.

"Agreed. One piece per day. That was the
rule for you three and that should be the rule
for Eden since she's living under our roof now,
and we also have to deal with the aftermath of

sugar highs. Something we haven't been exposed to in more years than we'll discuss."

Miranda dropped a plastic spider bracelet into the bucket and a mermaid toy for her collection.

"Thanks, Gwammy! I don't like candy. I like toys and juree," Eden said, beaming.

"She means jewelry," Roxie corrected. Everyone nodded.

"We know what she meant," Miranda said. "She'll get there. Jewelry is a hard word for a three-year-old isn't it, baby?"

Eden nodded as Sierra entered from the hall. "Is that Ariel from The Little Mermaid in our living room? May I have a hug, Miss Ariel?" Eden rushed over and Sierra knelt to squeeze her adorable niece.

"We'll be back by eight. This thing is going past her bedtime, but that's what holidays are for. Remember our Halloween antics, Sierra? We would sneak candy into our room and hide it under our pillows."

"Yes, I remember. The tooth fairy always seemed to come for one of us shortly thereafter. Usually, it was for you. I remember Mom finding tootsie rolls under your pillow after she'd already caught you the night before with some other candy. I knew you were going to be in big trouble, so I said they were mine and that I hid them under your pillow."

"I guess you had your moments," Roxie teased.

"I knew that candy was Roxie's," Miranda

lamented. "You two had been arguing about something or other that entire night before, so when you covered for her, I let it go. It was worth it to stop the fussing between you two."

"Some things haven't changed. You two still seem to butt heads over the smallest things," Richard added. "But remember who's there for you when the chips are down. Family. Sisters. Even your knucklehead brother." Sierra and Roxie exchanged smiles of understanding. They knew their father only spoke the truth.

"Mama, let's go!" Eden tugged at Roxie's black leggings.

"Okay, sweetie. See you all later on. Pray for me to get through the next two hours with all of the kids under the age of ten in Mill Hollows."

****

Poppy stretched her legs across the edge of the couch and perched her fluffy body alongside Richard. A knock at the door alerted her attention as she raised her head and her eyes darted around.

"It's alright, Poppy. It's Wes. You know

Wes. He's the one with a little bit of fuzzy hair on his face like you," Richard joked.

"Ha. Ha. Very funny, Dad." Sierra opened the door and welcomed Wes inside.

"Hey. Happy Halloween everyone," Wes said as he walked over and petted Poppy, who had risen with her tail in the air awaiting him.

"Happy Halloween. We're hanging out and watching the news. We will be watching Charlie Brown on the tube in a bit when Eden gets back. That's our big Halloween plan," Richard said.

"Wes, there's some warm apple cider in the kitchen on the stove. You and Sierra have some please before heading off to wherever you're going," Miranda offered.

"We're just going to dinner at Hill's Italian Eatery. No big plans. Neither of us is really into adult Halloween antics at Frankie's Brewhaus or Pollyanna's Dance Hall," Sierra said.

"Pollyanna's is now a hangout for more kids your age. They dropped Dance Hall from the name a few years ago," Miranda added. "Your dad and I used to cut a rug and a half down there when you all first moved out. The crowd changed as us line dancers and shaggers stopped going."

After a shared cup of apple cider, Sierra and Wes were on their way to dinner.

"I have something for you," Wes said after they had ordered.

"For moi? What is it?" Sierra teased.

Wes placed a small box on the table. "I found this by the gristmill and cleaned it up. A blue quartz that has molded into this shape over time as it rested upon a large buried formation."

"It's shaped almost like a heart. Wow. I love it, Wes!" Sierra rubbed her fingers over it, admiring the rare shape it had formed into.

"I find all sorts of things in my line of work. I found a diamond on a dig in Murfreesboro, Arkansas. I've had it cleaned and kept it in a safe deposit box. It's roughly a carat."

"This is lovely. Thank you so much for giving this to me."

After dinner, a nervous Wes walked Sierra to her front porch and took her by the hand.

"May we sit? There's something I need to tell you."

Sierra's throat tightened. "What is it? I don't think I want to know."

Wes dampened his lips and breathed in deeply as they found a seat on the steps. "I've got an opportunity. It means that I'd have to end my contract earlier than anticipated."

"How soon?" Sierra asked hesitantly.

"It's a position with a company working on a dig in Africa. It's six months in two different countries in Africa. I've been before, but only for a few weeks. It's something I would've jumped on before coming here, but now. The rush of an exploratory dig doesn't thrill me in the same way. I'm not sure what I'm going to do. I thought I should tell you right away, so it doesn't..."

"Doesn't blindside me when you leave? I'm sorry. It's a great opportunity for you, Wes. I would never ask you to even consider turning something like that down. That's a once-in-a-lifetime offer."

"It is. I thoroughly enjoyed my time there in college. My life is different than it was then. My goals are changing. I've spent all of my twenties on the road and moving around. I really need to consider this. It's not like I have a job offer after my contract ends to stay here, but you're here. I need to know what you want. Do you see a future with me if I found a way to stay in Mill Hollows or would you go with me if my career takes me elsewhere?"

"That's a loaded set of questions. I can't be the reason you stay. I just can't. Do I love you? Absolutely. Do I want you to stay or would I go with you elsewhere? Yes to both. But I'm not the one with a chance of a lifetime career-wise in front of me. You are."

Sierra stood up and folded her arms. Wes put his hands in his pockets and searched for words or the right move to make.

"It's chilly. I should get inside. You don't even have a coat on. We can talk about this later." Sierra knew she didn't have the right to be angry, but she couldn't ignore the sensation of being kicked in the stomach repeatedly at the thought of losing Wes.

"I don't want to leave like this, Sierra. I can tell you're hurting. I'm hurting."

"What do you want me to say, Wes? I haven't decided on my plans. How can I ask you to make commitments to me? We've only known each other for a short time. Life's short. Do what makes you happy. Going to Africa would make the Wes I've come to know quite happy."

"Okay. I guess I thought we would make decisions together, but you're exactly right. Life is short. And I must not make you happy enough for you to ask me to stay."

With that, Wes turned and walked away. He didn't look back and Sierra turned and walked inside, fighting back tears until she reached her room and closed the door. Her parents had retired to their room and Roxie was putting Eden to bed. She didn't want anyone to hear her cry. There had been enough tears cried on pillows already since her return by her sister. She didn't want to give anyone a reason to feel sorry for her. She knew when she got involved with Wes that he would likely be leaving, and she let her guard down anyway. She had planned on telling him that she had decided to stay and run the cafe. There was no reason to tell him now. She couldn't hold him back.

Roxie opened the door quietly and sat down on the bed beside Sierra, who was foiled into the fetal position with her head on a pillow. Roxie laid down behind Sierra and wrapped her arm around her sister's waist.

"Is Eden asleep?" Sierra asked with a

muffled voice.

"Yes. She's worn out. My little mermaid is counting fish in her sleep. I'm here. Tell me about this tomorrow. For now, go to sleep. I've got you, sis."

CHAPTER EIGHTEEN

The first day of November brought about a flurry of patrons to the Salted Caramel Cafe. Menu items including turkey and dressing to welcome the first day of November had always been a crowd-pleaser. Cranberry scones and slices of pumpkin pie were already close to selling out and the lunch rush hadn't even ended. The entire Blake family was on hand to welcome the start of the Thanksgiving season. Visitors touring the Blue Ridge mountains had found their way over from Roanoke and neighboring towns to Mill Hollows for stops at historical sites and quaint shops. The cafe was a favorite of locals, but also travelers.

Roxie and Miranda prepared casseroles and side dishes. Richard and Tom carved slices of turkey and ham. Sierra and Carlotta were covered in flour and frosting from working on baked goods and desserts. Eden had stayed with a sitter, who was to play with her dolls and have a tea party.

As the crowd began to wind down, Richard and Tom slipped out the back door and over to the sports bar to watch the Virginia Tech game against a top rival.

"I see your dad and Tom have disappeared. That seems to happen every year that we have a family work weekend during football season," Miranda remarked. "I don't suppose I'd have it any other way. It wouldn't be the same if those two didn't sneak across to grab a beer together and watch the game."

"I think we should all head over. I don't understand why we aren't allowed to attend a game where Tom's coaching," Sierra said.

"We'll jinx him," Roxie said. "That's what he says. We went once last year during his first year of coaching and they lost. I mean, they really lost. It was the only home game they had lost so far in the season. After that, they went on to win the remaining home game. That was it. Their season hasn't been great this year, so you know. We'd only add to the losing streak if we attended."

"Well, you girls are the same way. Roxie, you wouldn't let me make an appointment to have my hair done by you because you said it would make you nervous. Sierra, when we visited you in Florida, you had us stay with you rather than putting us up in that swanky resort you worked at because you were afraid we'd complain too much to the front desk." Miranda always had the words for putting one in his or her place.

The women pursed their lips and nodded at their mother, as each began wiping down their stations. Roxie whistled and Sierra cleared her throat. A hearty chuckle ensued by all as

Miranda strutted past them. They enjoyed seeing their mother in her element, teasing her children, and smiling with contentment. She had been through so much, and to see her come out stronger was more than admirable to them.

"Things look good here. Let's go catch the final quarter," Miranda said, shutting off the lights.

As they exited the door, Sierra hung back. "I'll be over in a minute. Go on ahead."

"Everything alright, Sierra?" Miranda asked.

"Do you need me to stay and help you with anything?" Roxie added with a curious head tilt. She was worried about her sister and they hadn't had a chance to discuss the tear-stained pillow incident from the night before.

"I'm good. I just need to pack up some cranberries to make some tea later on at home," Sierra said to persuade them to leave. She nodded at Roxie to go ahead with Miranda.

Sierra leaned back on a table in the front of the cafe and slid onto it. She surveyed the room. There needed to be a few cornucopias added to the tables to hold silverware and napkins. It was time to remove the witch from the shelf in the corner. She thought of menu items to add for the upcoming holiday season.

This is what I want. I want to manage the cafe. I can do it all. Cook. Bake. Handle the budgeting and finances. Marketing. I'm going to do it. Roxie doesn't want to do this and she stepped up when I couldn't. How did I never consider taking over the cafe before? I've always loved it. I know what I didn't love. Small country towns. I wanted to leave this place behind. Now, I can't imagine anywhere else I'd rather be...unless it were with...Wes.

CHAPTER NINETEEN

Sierra drove up to the cabin; anxiousness filling her chest. Wes' truck wasn't there. She got out and walked to the door, holding an envelope in her shaky hand. After knocking to be sure he wasn't home, she took the spare key and went inside. She laid the envelope on the table for Wes to read the contents upon his return.

Wes,
Whatever you choose to do. Whatever path you need to take. I hope you'll remember me and our time together. Though it was short, my feelings for you are the kind you hold onto forever. I couldn't ask you to stay but know that I want you to. You've found one-of-a-kind objects along your travels, but the truth is you're one-of-a-kind, also. I'm here to stay. In case you're wondering how to find me, should you ever choose to keep in touch, I'll be here at the cabin. You said it feels like home to you here. I'm going to move in here. It will keep some part of you close because you feel like home to me.
Love,
Sierra

CHAPTER TWENTY

Richard was taking off his boots in the mudroom as Sierra entered the back door.

"Need help, Dad?"

"Naw, I got it. I'm sorry things didn't work out for you and Wes, Sugar. He seemed a little choked up when he gave me the keys earlier."

"What?! He's already gone? He didn't tell me he was leaving right away."

"He'll be back this weekend to get his belongings. He had a meeting in Richmond with the Corps of Engineers. I guess he's filling out paperwork to complete his assignment."

Sierra breathed a small sigh of relief at knowing he hadn't left yet. Perhaps, she'd see him once more, but then again, it was probably for the best if she didn't. He could read her letter, and go chase his dreams. That's all she wanted for him was happiness. That once-in-a-lifetime experience that awaited. The joy she had experienced being with him.

CHAPTER TWENTY-ONE

Roxie arrived home with Eden to hear the roaring of a mixer and smell the sweetness of apple spice coming from the kitchen. Eden raced into the kitchen to find Sierra with an apron and hair twisted into a ponytail, visible through the strap of a Virginia Tech baseball cap.

"Aunt Rie!" Eden screamed in excitement. "Whatcha makin'?"

Sierra shut off the mixer and washed her hands in the sink. "I'm trying a new apple casserole idea out for the cafe. It will have baked apples cut in halves along the bottom, layered with stuffing in between each apple. See, this is half of the apple. There is the other half. Both are the same size. If you pushed them back together, you'd have the whole apple."

"Teaching a little fractions to a three-year-old, are ya?" Roxie chuckled.

"You're never too young to learn math, sis. I started teaching you how to add as soon as I learned."

"I'm sure you taught me more about subtraction. Like, when you would *take away* a cookie from my snack plate. Even now,

115

you've *removed* Tom's old baseball cap from the closet."

They snickered as Eden ran over to the mudroom and grabbed a boot belonging to Richard.

"Mama, if I take Gwandpa's shoe and hide it, he will have one shoe. Not two."

"That's right, baby. You're so smart. My child is a genius," Roxie said as she picked Eden up and placed her on her hip, kissing her cheeks and nose, as Eden giggled.

She put her down as Miranda came in from volunteering at the museum and Eden ran to hug her grandmother.

"Hey, my favorite girl. Did you have a good day at school?"

"Yes, Gwammie. I made a turkey wif my hand," she said raising her hand and playing with her fingers."

"I can't wait to put it on the fridge," Miranda said with pride.

"Girls, have you heard about Dalton Mill? They've gotten the approval to make it a historical site and will be doing some renovations within the codes of what you can do with a historic site, that is."

"That's why Wes was here. He was testing soil and other elements around the mill. It was all part of the process in getting that area designated as a landmark and for safety regulations," Sierra said, as her throat thickened with thoughts of Wes.

"Right. Well, the town is going to get

special use permits to use it for the museum. That will be a much better site for the arrowhead collections and artifacts we currently showcase in the back of Kinder's Jewelry. I've been asked to work as the Volunteer Coordinator and I get a few perks with that. I'm over the moon at being part of it. I have fond memories with your father and you kids down by those trails. I grew up when the mill was still in use. I've hated watching it sit for the last thirty years."

"That's awesome, Mom," Sierra said. "I'm glad Wes got to be a part of restoring our town in some way. Whatever I can do to help, I'm in. I've decided to stick around."

"Well, if you're going to work more at the museum when it opens and if Sierra's going to be staying....how would you feel about me bowing out of the cafe? I mean, I will still help out. I just really need something that gives me a reason to smile outside of Eden. I want to come home and be the best mom I can be to her, and I need a change for that to happen." Roxie sighed a heavy breath, as though she'd released the weight of the surrounding mountains from her shoulders.

Miranda and Sierra exchanged looks of mutual agreement.

"I'd love to run the cafe. I have so many ideas for sprucing up the ambiance and a few new dishes and desserts I'd like to try out. I'm bursting with ideas for making the Salted Caramel Cafe live up to its name. Maybe even a competition or two again can be in the works. I'd love to drizzle up some goodness."

"Sierra, please. You don't need to market to us. Please take over the cafe. Just no cornball advertising for us. Save it for the customers," Roxie said with her finger over her tongue, followed by a sparkling twinkle in her eyes and a spirited laugh Sierra and Miranda hadn't heard in ages.

"It's settled. Sierra's going to manage the cafe. I'm going to work at the museum, and Roxie, what are you planning to do if you leave the cafe?" Miranda inquired. "I've always known this was temporary for you. Managing the cafe was never meant to be your career. I hope you don't think I expected you to do it forever. I've just been waiting for you to come to me and tell me you were ready to move on."

"I stayed because you needed me. I was angry with you, Sierra, for not coming back. I know I've said harsh things in the past, but it's because I was scared. I was afraid I'd be the downfall of the cafe. I needed my sister and I blamed you for putting me in the position to take over. The truth is, it's exactly what I needed. I discovered I can handle so much more than I gave myself credit for in the past. I've needed the cafe as my escape from all of the drama with Toby and now, I appreciate the time I've had learning how to become more of a people person, which we all know I never really was. I think I'm ready to go back to working in a salon again. I'm wiser and more self-assured. I also am less likely to want to give someone a mullet if they complain."

Each of them moved forward and embraced. Tears stained their cheeks. Tears of sadness and letting go of the negative obstacles. Cancer. Failed relationships. Career slides. They had come out stronger on the other side. Tears of sadness became chuckles of joy.

Eden ran up and squeezed her tiny body into the middle of the circle they had formed. The laughter grew louder.

"I thought you were on the couch playing Barbies," Sierra said.

"I was. My Barbies are hugging too."

CHAPTER TWENTY-TWO

Laughter and love were abound at the Salted Caramel Cafe, where the Blake family gathered with a few of the local business owners for an annual pre-Thanksgiving meal. Gratitude and Gravy was the theme of invitations for the gathering. Sierra had created the humorous alliterative title. Guests remarked on how they'd shared the invitations with friends and the community. A turkey with silverware in his hands sitting in a bowl of gravy had resonated just as Sierra had hoped. It would be memorable and thus, increase customers.

"Sierra, your marketing ideas have never failed our family business. Your suggestion years ago to change the name after winning a contest for salted caramel cheesecake had me skeptical, but it turned out to increase our business tenfold. Especially, in the glorious season of Autumn," Miranda said, leaning over to Sierra as they checked the tray of mini apple pies that would be shared for dessert.

"Thanks, Mom. I appreciate the confidence in me. I'm going to do my best to make you proud," Sierra replied.

"Dear, I'm always proud of my children. I have no doubt you'll make the cafe even better than I have and you know I'll be checking in on you to make sure."

"Oh, I know you will."

Miranda patted Sierra on the shoulder.

As grace had been led by Richard and a gratitude round had been shared by most, Sierra and Roxie exchanged smiles of mutual respect and admiration.

"I'm grateful for so many things," Sierra began. "My family, who bring out my creativity and confidence, are gifts that I am eternally grateful for. Even though life doesn't go as planned most of the time, I'm also grateful for someone I met recently who reminded me of why I love our little town."

She noticed the crowd's attention had shifted toward the entrance behind her. The chime of the door opening sent shockwaves over her, as she slowly turned around. Wes smiled as he raised one hand and waved casually toward everyone. He made his way toward Sierra as she met him in the aisle.

"Hey. I'm sorry to interrupt. I got your note. I took a chance that you may be here. I had no idea I was walking in on a community audience of eyes and ears," Wes said.

"Come on in and grab a chair," Richard said with a husky voice, sliding a chair out from the table. "The more, the merrier."

Sierra caught her breath. "I thought you left. I left that note last week when you were in

Richmond. I haven't seen your truck there since. I assumed you'd gone back to Colorado."

Everyone continued to stare, as they took small bites and unconvincingly looked around the room.

"I did. I had some soul-searching to do. When I got your note, all I wanted to do was see you, but I needed to figure some things out. I was in Richmond discussing my findings and submitting final reports for the historical project. While there, I was offered a full-time position with the Corps of Engineers as a staff geologist. I called them yesterday and accepted. Calling you didn't seem nearly enough, so I got a red eye last night."

Sierra felt her eyes begin to moisten and her heartbeat fasten. "So, you're staying?"

"Someone said I should take chances on things that happen once in a lifetime. I don't need to search the world to find what is standing right in front of me. Falling in love with you is *my* once-in-a-lifetime experience. Of all the gems I've found along the way, you're the best one of all."

"Son, are you ever going to kiss her? This dinner theater show needs a finale' so we can eat dessert," Richard said with a hearty chortle.

"Yes, sir. As the locals say, I'd be much obliged."

"Don't ever say that again," Sierra said as smiles filled their cheeks and Wes pulled her into his arms. Everyone clapped and raised their glasses, cheering them on.

EPILOGUE

ONE YEAR LATER

The inauguration of Dalton Mill as a historical landmark had the residents of Mill Hollows gathered along the newly cleared trail. A few trees had been removed to allow for a clear view of the renovated mill; now home to the Mill Hollows Museum. The faded red watermill had been painted to freshen the coat to a vibrant apple red; providing tranquility as it slowly churned in the water.

Miranda Blake presided over the event, discussing some of the artifacts of local and regional history on display. Faded photographs hung along the walls of town founders and former leaders. A gem collection of quartz, garnet, and other rock formations, gems, and minerals were in a display case from Wes' collection.

After the ceremony, Wes and Sierra took a walk down to the waterfall further down the trail. Water rushed in fury down the lower mountain and into the Roanoke River on its descent toward Smith Mountain Lake.

"This is so beautiful. With the trails ending about 50 feet back, I've never been in clear view of the waterfall. It's breathtakingly serene. Magical," Sierra said in awe of the landscape surrounding them.

"I pitched hard for the clearing to include a path closer to this. It was a shame people were missing out on such beauty," Wes added.

He reached his arms around Sierra's waist and leaned his head around hers. Sierra could feel his thin beard brush against her cheek.

"I've seen many beautiful places, but with you by my side, every place I see is even more radiant," Wes said as he turned Sierra toward him.

"I once found a diamond hidden in obscurity and thought nothing else would sparkle as much as that stone. Now, I've found a diamond with even more dazzle to the eye and into the soul. You."

Wes reached into his pocket and lowered down on one knee upon a large rock. He pulled out the diamond he'd found in Arkansas and reached for Sierra's left hand. Tears filled her eyes and her cheeks began to ache with anticipation.

"Will you stand with me along the rocky roads of life and search beside me for the gems yet to be discovered? You're my heart. My love. And my home. Will you marry me?"

Sierra's body quivered as she nodded her head. Wes raised to meet her eyes.

"Yes! Yes! A thousand times, yes!" Wes slid the ring onto her finger, as tears began to fill his eyes. Sierra threw her arms around his shoulders and he squeezed her into him. As they slowly released from their embrace, Wes leaned Sierra back into a dip as he'd done by the covered bridge soon after they'd met.

"I wanted to kiss you so badly the last time I leaned you over my arms like this."

"I wanted your kiss then, and I want your kiss now," Sierra replied, as he pulled her back up into his arms and lips on lips.

THE END

ABOUT THE AUTHOR

Angie Ellington is a novelist from NC.

She enjoys writing contemporary women's fiction and romance. Titles are available in ebook, print (standard & large print) via Amazon. They are also available in audiobook via Audible & Apple.

If you enjoyed this book, please leave a review on the retailer site you purchased from, and/or Goodreads or Bookbub.

www.angienellington.com

Christmas in Frost Bend
Autumn at Apple Hill
Spring in Lilac Glen

Carlisle Bay Series
Dancing by the Moonlight
Dancing by the Christmas Lights

PREVIEW OF

CHRISTMAS IN FROST BEND

Chapter One

Summer-- 10 years ago

"I wanted to tell you last week, but with everything going on with graduation and you leaving early to go back home, I decided to wait until I could tell you face to face." Lacey Myers was trembling with emotions while telling her boyfriend of five years that she had accepted a paid internship with a large retail chain based in Boston. She wasn't sure if it was the right decision, but she knew she'd regret it if she didn't see this through.

"When did you apply for a job in Boston? I thought you were all set to start as a junior designer with Celine's?" (Celine's was an interior design firm based in Charlotte about an hour from their hometown of Frost Bend, North Carolina).

"When did this happen? I know things aren't going exactly as planned for us, but I thought we at least still agreed that our future was together." Mason Peters was feeling deflated. Like he had been hit by a truck. He didn't know how to respond to this. A job offer in Boston and a move several states away. This was not what they had planned after college graduation. They had discussed marriage and moving in together after college. That had always been the plan.

Lacey fought back tears. "Everything just happened so quickly. I found out about the position in my final lecture from our T.A. I was only mulling it over to discuss with you when you shared the news of your grandfather's cancer diagnosis and that your dad needed you to move back home to help with the electrical business. We had discussed moving to Charlotte, but not back to Frost Bend." Lacey couldn't stop herself and before she could stop the words, they spilled out abruptly. "Small towns are not going to give either of us the opportunities we need at this stage of our lives and the career goals we have. At least not my career goals. You wanted to be an engineer. Not settle and be an electrician. I—I didn't mean that. Mason, I don't mean to criticize you." She wished she could take that back. It just came out. The guilt and sadness of leaving Mason were overwhelming her, but she had to do what was best for her. She was only twenty-two years old. She couldn't make her plans based on her boyfriend's choices. She wanted more.

Their lives had been a bubble in college.

They had been together since their senior year of high school and friends since they were kids. It was time to take chances that didn't include each other. She wanted to be an interior designer, but that was a long way off. If she worked at Celine's, she wouldn't have the opportunities she could have with a large corporation. Perhaps, becoming an interior designer and owning her own firm may not happen, but she would gain respect and connections in a large market. That's how she would make a name for herself. She needed to prove herself. That would not happen in Frost Bend. She didn't want to resent Mason for being the reason she didn't take this opportunity and truth be told, moving to Charlotte was settling for Lacey. She wanted to experience new things. She needed to find out if there was more for her than getting married after college and working in a mediocre position.

"I'm sorry, Mason. I know you are doing what is best for your family. That's one of the things I love most about you; your commitment to family and ability to take charge when people need you. I just...I'm not ready for the same life that I think you are. Not right now. You'll be happy back home. I won't be. Not if I don't see for myself where this could lead for me." Lacey sighed heavily. She had stood her ground. She had convinced herself she was making the right choice. At least mostly.

"The same life? I thought being together was what you wanted. Moving forward after college together. Supporting each other. I've always supported your dreams. I just can't support you following them so far away; at least not now when I'm committed to helping my family with the business. I guess I just didn't expect you to choose a career first. I wouldn't ask you to choose me first either. I...I guess I assumed—hoped... you would at least choose opportunities that could benefit you *with* me...not *without*."

Mason felt his heart sink into his chest and knew by the look on Lacey's face that her mind was made up. He would be wasting his breath to try and convince her to stay. If he had to convince her, it wasn't meant to be. He had to let her go. She was meant for bigger things. Traveling, expensive things, and someone who could provide her with what she wanted to be happy, even if it wasn't what she necessarily needed. He could see Lacey had changed. She wanted different things and he wasn't part of her plans anymore.

"You do what you need to, Lacey. If moving to Boston is what your heart is telling you to do...thcn it's what you should do. I've never wanted to be the guy who stood in the way of your dreams. I would never make you happy if you stayed. Not now. You're right. You would resent me and so would I because I'd wonder if *we* were...if *I* were enough."

Two weeks later, Lacey moved to Boston.

She had second-guessed herself enough. She had to find out what she truly wanted. Mason was right. They wouldn't have been happy if she had stayed. She had to follow a path of her own. So did he. They stayed in touch for a while, but eventually, all communication ended.

Love at the Salted Caramel Cafe

Angie Ellington

Love at the Salted Caramel Cafe

Made in the USA
Middletown, DE
26 September 2023

39428113R00080